THE GLENCOE LITERATURE LIBRARY

High Elk's Treasure

and Related Readings

Glencoe
McGraw-Hill

New York, New York   Columbus, Ohio   Woodland Hills, California   Peoria, Illinois

Acknowledgments

Grateful acknowledgment is given authors, publishers, photographers, museums, and agents for permission to reprint the following copyrighted material. Every effort has been made to determine copyright owners. In case of any omissions, the Publisher will be pleased to make suitable acknowledgments in future editions.

HIGH ELK'S TREASURE, by Virginia Driving Hawk Sneve. Copyright © 1972 by Virginia Driving Hawk Sneve. All rights reserved.

"The War for the Black Hills" from *Bury My Heart at Wounded Knee: An Indian History of the American West* by Dee Brown. Copyright © 1970 by Dee Brown. Published by Henry Holt and Company, Inc. New York. Reprinted by permission.

"The Call of the Wild Horses" from THE MAN WHO LISTENS TO HORSES by Monty Roberts. Copyright © 1996, 1997 by Monty Roberts. Reprinted by permission of Random House, Inc.

Poem, "The Legacy II" by Leroy V. Quintana. Reprinted by permission of the author.

"Lineage" from *This Is My Century: New and Collected Poems* by Margaret Walker Alexander. Copyright © 1989 by Margaret Walker Alexander. Reprinted by permission of the University of Georgia Press.

"A Legend of Devil's Tower" from AMERICAN INDIAN MYTHS AND LEGENDS by Richard Erdoes and Alfonso Ortiz. Copyright © 1984 by Richard Erdoes and Alfonso Ortiz. Reprinted by permission of Pantheon Books, a division of Random House, Inc.

Cover Art: Courtesy of Wild Wings, Inc. Lake City, MN 55041

Glencoe/McGraw-Hill

A Division of The **McGraw·Hill** Companies

Send all inquiries to:
Glencoe/McGraw-Hill
8787 Orion Place
Columbus, OH 43240

ISBN 0-07-820366-X
Printed in the United States of America
2 3 4 5 6 7 8 9 026 04 03 02 01 00

Contents

High Elk's Treasure

Author's Note   vi

Glossary   vii

OTOKAHE, The Beginning   1

The Lost Filly   7

High Elk's Cave   11

One Hundred Years   15

Wild Horse Catchers!   22

The Rescue   28

Howard High Elk   33

Joe and Howard   39

The High Elk Treasure   44

Related Readings   49

Dee Brown   from *The War for the Black Hills*   historical nonfiction   50

Continued

Contents *continued*

Monty Roberts   from **The Man Who Listens**   informative   **57**
                 to Horses   nonfiction

Leroy V. Quintana   **The Legacy II**   poem   **68**

Margaret Walker   **Lineage**   poem   **69**

as told by   **A Legend of Devil's Tower**   folktale   **70**
Lame Deer

Jean Fritz   from **Homesick: My Own Story**   memoir   **74**

iv

High Elk's Treasure

Virginia Driving Hawk Sneve

Author's Note

THE STORY, PLACES, AND CHARACTERS in this book are fictitious, with the exception of General Custer, his brother, and the Sioux warrior, Rain-In-The-Face.

The Battle of the Little Big Horn is recorded historically; but the manner of General Custer's death has never been authenticated. I make no claim to any new or specific knowledge of the General's death.

My thanks to my grandmother, Flora Driving Hawk, and to Mr. and Mrs. Emmet Jones for their assistance in the spelling, definition, and pronunciation of Sioux words.

Virginia Driving Hawk Sneve

Glossary with Phonetic Pronunciation

INA (*eeh-nah*): my mother

IYOPTE (*ee-yo-ptay*, the *p* is an exploded sound not found in English): get going

LAKOTA or DAKOTA: what the Sioux called themselves, meaning friendly people

NIYE (*nee-yea*): you

OH HINH: exclamation of shock, surprise or fear. Similar to "Oh dear" in English

OTOKAHE (*oh-toe-kaw-hey*): beginning

PARFLECHE (*par-flesh*): a case made of rawhide with the hair removed

PILAMIYE or PIDAMIYE (*pee-la-me-yea*): thank you

SIOUX (*soo*): Early French settlers first gave the Dakota this name, taken from the Chippewa "Nadowessi" which means poisonous snake, or enemy. The French changed the spelling to "Nadowessioux" which was in time shortened to Sioux.

ŚUNGWIYE (*shoong-we-yea*): mare

TAKOZA (*tah-ko-zha*): grandchild

TEĤINDA (*tay-hin-dah*, the *h* is sounded as in the *ch* of the German "ach"): forbid, taboo

TIPI (*tee-pee*): a cone-shaped tent of animal skins, used by the Plains Indians

TRAVOIS (*tr-voy*): a sledge used by the Plains Indians, consisting of a net or platform dragged along the ground on two poles that support it and serve as shafts for the horse or dog pulling it

UN (*oon*, second person singular of the verb "to be"): are

UNCI (*oon-chee*): my grandmother

WANAǴI (*wah-nah-gee*, the g is a guttural sound not found in English): get going

WAŚICUN or WAŚICU (*wah-she-choon*): white man, white woman, white person

OTOKAHE, The Beginning

*I*N THE AUTUMN OF THE YEAR *1876, a harried band of Brulé Sioux gave up their freedom and permanently settled on the Dakota reservation which had been set aside for them. They had been part of the huge encampment of Sioux and Cheyenne which had defeated General Custer at the Battle of the Little Big Horn on June 25, 1876. Unable to hunt game, constantly hounded by the United States Army and forced to hide, they came to the hated reservation because they could no longer defend themselves and they were starving.*

Among this pitiful little band was a youth called High Elk. He was in the beginning of his manhood, seething with rage at the white men who were destroying his people and who had killed his father. High Elk came only because his mother was ill and desperately needed a place to rest and regain her health. He walked to the reservation, leading an old, scrawny palomino on which his mother rode. The mare was too lame to be ridden far, and was barely able to pull a travois holding their tipi and a few personal belongings.

The mare, her rib and hip bones sharply protruding, was permanently lamed. Her coat was ragged and much of her mane and tail were gone. She didn't look strong enough to pull the travois and she stumbled as she walked. Perhaps this was why the soldiers let High Elk keep her.

High Elk (whose name had originally been Steps-High-Like-An-Elk) loved horses, as did all of the Sioux. Sioux horsemen had been the bravest, most daring, and most agile of all the Plains Indians. Horses were the Sioux's wealth and their whole life style was built around the mobility which the animals provided them.

High Elk had plans for his mare and tethered her near the tipi. As the animal grazed bare all of the grass around, he moved the tipi. He had to watch over the mare at all times, for starving Indians might try to steal her for food. Even High Elk's mother felt that the horse should be slaughtered to provide them with meat.

Still High Elk kept the mare. He let no one but himself handle her, and he did dangerous things to ensure her healthy survival. Under the cover of night he would often slip into the agency stables to steal oats for her to eat. When her strength was revived and she fattened, he sneaked her into the agency corral and bred her to a great, golden quarter horse. This handsome animal belonged to the Agent who was building a herd of golden ponies with choice mares taken from the Indians. If this white man had seen High Elk's mare, now that she was in good condition again, he would have taken the horse in spite of her lame leg. So High Elk used every precaution to hide his treasure.

The mare bore a beautiful filly with the golden color of her sire and the white face and stockings of her dam. The filly thrived, and once more High Elk bred the palomino to the same stud.

As he was sneaking the mare out of the corral the guards discovered him. Thinking that he was trying to steal a horse to eat, they shot at him. Even though High Elk's right leg was shattered, he managed to mount the lame mare and ride safely home. He knew that he dare not stay in the open with a wounded leg since he was now unable to protect his mother or his horses. So High Elk and his mother moved to the bank of a creek where a large, shallow cave provided shelter and sanctuary for them. The thickly wooded bank concealed the opening of the cave and they remained undiscovered. The mare safely bore a colt and the herd was begun.

In 1887 the federal government passed the General Allotment Act, and High Elk and his mother each received 160 acres of land which bordered the creek on both sides. He was able to take the horses out of hiding. After his mother died, High Elk married. He and his wife had two sons who were alloted 60 acres each. With the additional land High Elk increased the size of his herd. The boys, in their teens, became skilled at capturing the wild mustang mares which High Elk selected to be bred into his herd. High Elk could no longer ride in the hunt, but would supervise from atop the Bald Peak on the Lodge Pole Ridge while his sons chased the wild ponies below.

By the time High Elk died, his horses had become famous for their beauty and for their ability to endure the harsh weather of the plains. Their speed and weight were also ideal for ranch work, and High Elk had begun to make money on the sale of his horses.

After High Elk's death his two sons quarreled and Howard sold his share of the horses and land and left the reservation. John, the second son, continued to operate the ranch. Then in the 1920's and early 30's the market for horses fell. The herd, the only source of the High Elks' income, decreased. Many of the horses were sold cheaply and others ran with the wild mustangs.

William, High Elk's grandson, dreamed of rebuilding the herd. He refused to permit farming on land which had never been turned by a plow. William found work as a maintenance man at the agency and was able to support his parents and the one remaining mare, until his father died.

William always hoped someday to buy back the land which had been sold by his uncle, Howard High Elk, but the hope died when most of those acres were turned into a wildlife preserve and the rest used as grounds for the Bureau of Indian Affairs day school. His dreams of rebuilding the herd faded as the expenses grew with his young family. His mother, who lived with them, was an additional drain on his meager resources. There never seemed to be the money to start anew.

The one remaining mare that William raised had become a pet which his children rode to school. Even with just one horse left, William had paid the fee for services of a stud of the same line so that the strain would remain pure. This last remaining mare had borne a filly, and would soon foal again. The High Elks all hoped the new foal would be a male so that the herd would have a fresh beginning.

William's son, thirteen-year-old Joe, had heard the tales of the High Elk horses all of his life. He longed for the day when the great heard could be started again.

High Elk's
Treasure

The Lost Filly

Joe High Elk looked out of the window as he stood in line with the other seventh and eighth grade students. He wondered why school was being dismissed early today. The sky was just as blue as it had been an hour ago when they had returned to class after lunch. Early dismissals seldom took place in the spring. It wasn't unusual to be let out right after lunch on some days in the winter, when the prairies on the Indian reservation were often swept by blizzards, but not this late in May. The students speculated noisily among themselves.

Mr. Gray Bear rapped on his desk to get his pupils' attention again. "We've had a phone call from the police that a tornado was sighted over by Lodge Pole Ridge. But," he quickly added to reassure those whose homes were in that area, "it did not touch down. We've had the radio on and there is a severe weather watch until five o'clock this evening. The buses will be here shortly, and I suggest that those of you who have over a mile to walk from your bus stop stay with friends until the storm danger is past. You students who walk or ride to school may leave if you don't have to cross the creek. If you do, then I'd like to have you stay here until the danger is over."

Mr. Gray Bear taught the seventh and eighth grades and was also principal of the consolidated elementary day school. Most of the students were bused in from the surrounding area and it would take at least an hour for many of them to get home. They began filing out of the room but Joe stopped at Mr. Gray Bear's desk.

"Mr. Gray Bear," Joe said. "I think Marie and I had better go on home. We have to go over the creek, but the place where we cross is practically dry."

Mr. Gray Bear put his hand on Joe's shoulder and guided the boy out of the room as they talked.

"It may be dry now, Joe, but if we get a hard rain you know how bad a flash flood can be."

"Yes, I know," answered Joe. "But our filly is fast and I'd like to get home before the storm strikes. Some of our stock is out and Grandma is home alone. She won't be able to round them up."

"Well, it's against my better judgment to let you go, but if you move right along you should be able to make it in time. Go ahead." Mr. Gray Bear understood the tall eighth grader's concern. Indian children often assumed adult responsibility at an early age.

Joe hurried outside to the back of the school where his horse, Star, was tethered. The horizon around was still clear blue. There was no sign of a storm cloud and he felt better. 'We'll make it home okay,' he thought, for he had stretched the truth just a little when he told Mr. Gray Bear that the stock was out. There was only the old mare, who was due to foal soon, and he wanted to make sure she was safe.

Maybe he was being reckless not staying safely at school especially since his little sister, Marie, would be riding double with him. But that unborn foal meant a lot to him.

Joe caught the filly and bridled her. She was nervous and danced away as he tried to mount her.

"Okay, girl, okay," he said soothingly. "I know the storm is coming. It's all right, Star, we'll make it home and see how your mama's doing." He calmed her, mounted and rode around to the front of the school where Marie was waiting.

"My teacher says we should stay here, Joe," she said, her black eyes sparkling with the fear and excitement she felt.

"We'll make it home in time, Marie. But we'll have to hurry. Come on."

Joe made a step of his foot and extended his hand to his ten-year-old sister. She was a tiny little girl and as Joe swung her up behind him her short legs stuck almost straight out on either side.

He turned the filly and urged her into a trot, and Marie tightened her arms around him to keep from bouncing off. They rode bareback because their father saved the family's only saddle for special occasions. He also felt that without a saddle there was less danger of the children being injured if they ever fell from the horse.

As they rode away from the shelter of the trees and buildings of the school and on to the open prairie, they saw the dark formation of thunderheads rising as high as the ridge in the west. Jagged streaks of lightning flashed continuously and they heard the thunder's rumble as the storm approached.

"Oh, Joe, I'm scared," Marie cried.

"We'll make it. Besides, you've been in storms before."

"I know," wailed his sister, "but not without Mom and Dad."

"Well, just hang on. I'm going to turn Star loose and you know how she likes to go!" Joe kicked Star into a gallop.

The filly, even with the combined weight of the two children, stretched out low to the ground. Marie's long braids flew behind her and the wind whistled in their ears as the horse sped over the level plain.

Almost at the creek, Joe reined Star in to check her before they went down the bank. But the filly knew she was going home and fought the bit.

"Hold on, Marie," Joe yelled. "She's not going to slow down!"

The sure-footed horse leapt down the narrow path to the creek with Joe and Marie lying low on her back to keep from being swiped off by the overhanging branches. Down they rode, splashed over the shallow stream, and started up the other side. The thunder cracked loudly, frightening the excited horse. She jumped, slipped in the mud and fell.

Joe, with Marie still tightly hanging on to his waist, threw himself clear of the falling horse. They landed, heavily, in a sumac bush just as the first fat drops of rain fell.

Joe jumped up and pulled Marie with him. "Are you hurt?" he asked.

"Yes," the little girl cried, "I'm bleeding!"

Blood was running down her arm and she was frightened at the sight of it.

"Here," Joe said, "wrap my handkerchief around your arm. It's only a scratch from the bush. It'll be okay. I've got to see how Star is."

The horse had scrambled to her feet and was calmly nibbling at the grass on the side of the path. Joe whistled to her and was horrified to see her limping as she came to him. The filly was favoring her right hind leg.

"Poor girl," Joe said, petting her and feeling for other injuries. Finding none, he took the horse's reins in one hand, Marie's hand in his other, and started up the bank.

"We have to get away from the creek, Marie," he yelled over the noise of the wind which had risen and was howling through the trees. "There may be a flash flood after it starts to rain."

He pulled the horse and the little girl after him and knew that they had to find shelter soon. The wind whipped the trees, and dry branches snapped and flew around them. There were blinding flashes of lightning followed by the loud crash of thunder. Marie stumbled and fell.

"Don't cry," Joe begged his sister as he helped her to her feet. "I'll let Star loose and carry you."

Quickly he slipped the bridle over the filly's head, wrapped and tied the reins around his waist and picked up the little girl.

"Where are we going, Joe?" asked Marie, clasping her arms tightly around his neck.

"To Grandpa's cave," he gasped. "Don't hang on so tight. You're choking me!"

Joe followed the steep path up the bank and paused to rest where the faintly discernible trail started to parallel the creek.

"You're too heavy, Marie," he panted. "If you can walk, we'll make better time. The rest of the way is level now."

The trail was covered with dead branches and leaves, but Joe knew the path and the cave well, for he often came to this place. He had been strangely drawn to the cave ever since he had been old enough to understand that it was here that the High Elk herd had its start. Even in the driving storm Joe easily found the cave's entrance, though it was well concealed by trees. He led Marie into the dry, leaf-carpeted cave and turned to urge Star, who had followed on the path, to enter.

The filly stood, peering curiously through the branches, but she ignored Joe's urging.

"Come on, Star," he said, trying to grab her mane, "get in out of the rain."

The rain had started in great blasting sheets and Joe heard the roar of the water in the creek, which indicated a flash flood.

The horse slipped from his grasp and trotted back along the path, heading home to the safety of her stall. Joe, unmindful of the rain, ran after her.

"Star!" he called. "Come back!" As he yelled, the frightened horse jumped as if shying at something and lost her footing on the wet path.

The bank crumpled beneath her and the filly slid into the rising waters of the creek. Now thoroughly bewildered, she splashed her way into the deeper channel and was swept downstream. Joe, helpless, saw her fighting the current of the flood. She broke free of the swiftly flowing waters and swam close to the far side, found her footing and scrambled out onto the bank. Joe gave a shout of relief at Star's safety, but then groaned in despair as she disappeared into the trees on the other side.

High Elk's Cave

Wет AND COLD, Joe sat hunched on his heels, hugging his knees and staring out of the mouth of the cave. The rain was still falling, but he could tell from the way the trees stood, quietly accepting the water, that the wind had died. The storm was almost over.

"Star is gone, Star is gone." Over and over he said the sad words to himself. How could the herd begin again when part of its hope was wandering, lost along the creek? Who knew how far the horse would go in her fright? And with her injured leg she would be easy prey for wolves or wildcats, predators willing enough to feed on a filly. Full of remorse and despair Joe sat ignoring Marie's attempt to cheer him up.

"Don't feel bad, Joe. You couldn't help it if that dumb Star wouldn't come into the cave. She's so dumb she didn't even know enough to slow down for the slippery trail. Don't feel bad. Even if we had stayed at school. . . ." Her voice faded away as she realized that these were not cheering words.

"Yeah!" Joe cried, jumping to his feet. "We should have stayed at school! I was the dumb one thinking I could get us home before the storm struck!" He grabbed up a branch lying on the floor and beat it against the wall of the cave crying, "Dumb! Dumb! Dumb!"

In his anger at himself Joe used all of his strength to swing the branch against the side of the cave. He swung, releasing his sorrow and fury while dirt and debris, gouged out of the wall, flew around him.

"Joe! Joe! Stop!" screamed Marie, dodging the wildly striking branch to grab his arm. She was frightened at his fury.

"Don't! Please, Joe! Stop!"

His anger spent, Joe gave one last heave of the branch and let it fall against the wall and to the floor. He stood, exhausted, arms hanging limply, staring, unseeing, at the wall.

He had struck repeatedly at the same spot and his wild, uncontrolled effort had dug a deep narrow hole in the wall. Looking at it he saw what he had done and was sad that in his anger he had desecrated the High Elk cave, which was a sacred place to him.

He futilely tried to erase the deep depression. As his hand smoothed the raw edges of the wound he felt a soft, crumbly substance which was not dirt. Looking closely, he cautiously explored the gap he had made.

"What is it, Joe?" asked Marie. "What have you found?"

"I don't know." His hands were quickly digging away at the earth, heedless of the further damage he was doing. "There is some object—leather I think—buried here."

He took the pocket knife he always carried and began to carefully carve around the bulky shape his hands had uncovered.

"See, Marie," he said. "There seems to be an old piece of leather wrapped around something."

Joe was excited now. As he dug he could see a rawhide bundle, old and rotten, that had been painstakingly tied with leather thongs.

Carefully, Joe freed it from its covering of dirt. Scraps of leather flaked off as he gently placed the bundle on the floor of the cave.

"What is it, Joe?" Marie asked. "Aren't you going to open it?"

"No," he answered. "It is too dark in here to see what it is. I need something to wrap it in so that it won't fall apart."

"Here," offered Marie, "use my sweater."

"No, I'll use my shirt. Your sweater will get all dirty."

"But your shirt is soaked. It'll get the whatever-it-is all wet," Marie said, placing her sweater on the floor of the cave.

"Well, I guess you're right, but I hope Mom doesn't get mad when she sees that your new sweater is dirty."

Gently and carefully, he moved the rawhide bundle and wrapped the sweater around it.

"This must be something that Grandpa buried here," Joe said, lifting the bundle into his arms.

"Grandpa?" queried Marie. "He never said anything about it."

"Not that grandpa," corrected Joe. "I mean our great-grandfather High Elk."

"Wow!" said Marie. "You mean that thing has been here since the time of our great grandfather? It really must be old."

"It is," answered Joe. "Don't you know that High Elk and his family lived here for a while?"

"Here?" said Marie, looking around at the dark, musty cave. "I thought he just kept his horses here."

"He did, but he lived in the same place so that he could always guard the horses."

"Oh, that must have been terrible!" exclaimed Marie. "I wouldn't like it at all."

Joe smiled. "You're spoiled. I bet you don't even remember when we lived in the old house without running water and electricity. Come on, we'd better head home. Grandma's probably worried about us."

The rain had stopped, but the water still dripped heavily from the trees.

"We'd better take our shoes off, Joe," Marie said, sitting down to remove hers. "They are the only ones we have and the mud will ruin them."

"Yeah," Joe agreed, admiring his little sister's practicalness, "I never thought of that."

They made a strange procession as they emerged from the cave. Joe, the reins wrapped around his waist with the bridle dangling and bumping against his thigh, walked barefooted. His jeans were rolled up, and he shivered as the water dripped on his already wet shirt. In his arms he carried, like a swaddled baby, the rawhide bundle carefully sheltered in Marie's sweater.

Marie followed lugging her shoes and his boots. Her long black hair, which had become unbraided, fell in tangled strands over her shoulders. She stepped carefully and distastefully along the wet, muddy path, trying to avoid soiling the full, gathered skirt of her dress.

"Careful now, Marie."

They had come to the place where the bank had crumbled under Star. The path had about a two-foot gap where the earth had fallen.

"Here, you'd better take my hand."

"I can't, Joe. My hands are full."

"Okay, I'll go first and then you hand me the shoes."

Joe's long legs easily stepped over the break. He laid the bundle down and then the shoes Marie handed him. He stretched out his hands to her and she trustingly took them. The little girl closed her eyes as she stepped across, not wanting to see the swirling, muddy, flood-filled creek below.

Safely on the firm path, the children picked up their bundles and walked up the bank, out of the trees and onto the open prairie.

They saw their house silhouetted against the gray bank of clouds which was streaked with the pink, white and blue rays of the setting sun.

Far to the left, the Lodge Pole Ridge stood like a dark wall casting its shadow for miles before it.

As they followed the trail, made by generations of horses going to water at the creek, they saw the lights come on in the house, and then the bright yard light illuminated the old horse shed and the path before them.

One Hundred Years

"*U*NCI," MARIE CALLED to her grandmother as she ran into the house.

"*Takoza*." Joe heard his grandmother's answer as he hurried, even though wet and cold, to the old shed to check on the mare. He knew Grandma would hear Marie's story of their wet adventure and he was not ready to face the scolding he knew she would give him. Grandma High Elk could understand English and spoke it when she had to; but to her grandchildren she spoke only *Lakota* and insisted that they speak it to her, so that they would know the Sioux tongue.

A soft nicker of greeting came from the shed as Joe neared it. The mare was there, safe from the storm. Joe was so relieved to find her unharmed that he put his arms around her neck and let the tears come. Quietly he sobbed into the mare's mane and she, puzzled by his strange behavior, nuzzled him gently with her lips.

"Śungwiye," he said her name quietly, slurring the guttural "g" of the word so that it was a gentle croon. "Śungwiye, will you still be my friend and give us our stallion? Oh, Śungwiye, I have been foolish. Your filly is lost."

Controlling his anguish, he did the evening chores for the mare. Her watering trough, which he usually filled, was overflowing with fresh rain water. He fed her the handful of oats which was her ration and filled the manger with hay. He stood back and watched with satisfaction as she ate. The colt was not yet ready to be born and the mare was healthy in her expectant state.

Joe heard the motor of his parents' car as it turned off the highway. He listened to the sound of its labor as it struggled through the wet, greasy gumbo of the ungraveled road. He hoped the car would not get stuck. His father would be angry enough at the loss of Star without adding the aggravation of a bogged-down automobile.

The High Elks' home was two miles from the main paved highway that crossed the reservation. The family could have had their new, government-built house erected on a lot in the agency town where both William and his wife, Marlene, worked. Then Joe and Marie could have walked to the agency school instead of having to ride double on the filly in the varying climate of the plains. But Grandma had refused to move to town. She said she would rather stay alone in the old log shanty that the first High Elk had built, where she had come as a bride and where her husband had died. William did not insist that his mother move to town, even though he and his wife would have an hour's drive to work. Also, in the back of his mind he was probably fearful that if he left the land, his dream of the High Elk horses would never be realized.

So the house was built next to the spot where the old home had stood for almost eighty-five years. Joe was glad. He loved the High Elk range bordered by the creek, the highway, and the Lodge Pole Ridge. He knew every foot of it and realized that it was unusual to find prairie ground untouched by a plow. Often, in the summer, William brought white men, historians from the state university, to view the grounds. They searched for Indian relics and listened attentively to William's proud recitation of his family's history. Joe learned early to share his father's pride in their homestead and wanted above all to make the land a working ranch with cattle and, of course, the horses.

Joe saw the car skid and slide in the clay-like gumbo and come to a stop. His parents got out and walked toward the house.

"Dad," he called to his father. "Dad, can I talk to you before you go in?"

William, carrying a bag of groceries in his arms, hesitated at his son's call.

Joe's mother, hearing the urgency in the boy's voice, said, "Here, Will, I'll take the groceries and start supper while you talk with Joe."

Unhappily, Joe watched his father's approach. How could he tell him what had happened? The boy's throat tightened. He was not afraid of his father, with whom he had always shared his every thought, but now Joe knew that what he had foolishly caused to happen would hurt his father, and he dreaded that more than a beating.

"Hi, Joe," greeted William, and then, seeing the empty stall beside Šungwiye, asked, "Where's Star?"

"She's lost, Dad," Joe said, miserably turning to hide his face against the high gate of the corral.

"Lost? What do you mean?" William demanded.

Quickly, Joe told of the early dismissal from school because of the storm warning and how he decided that he could get home before the storm struck; the wild ride over the creek, Star's fall and the injury to her leg; how he and Marie took shelter in the cave; and finally, the filly's plunge into the flooded creek and her disappearance on the opposite bank.

William was silent for a long minute before he said, "I know you realize the danger that Star is in, wandering the prairie. She's not even on familiar range. From your description of where she went into the trees, she must be on the wildlife preserve. We'll need permission to go in and hunt for her. Star may be hard to find if she joins the protected herd of wild horses, or if the predators frighten her into running off to the other end of the preserve."

"I know," Joe said miserably.

"I can't scold you, Joe. You should have known you needn't have worried about a wise old range mare like Sungwiye. She'd head for shelter when she first sensed the storm, long before a man would."

"All I could think about was the foal."

William nodded understandingly. "Well," he said, "there's nothing we can do tonight. When I get to work tomorrow I'll call the ranger on the preserve and ask him to be on the lookout for Star and get permission to hunt for her. We'll have to wait until Saturday to borrow horses and organize a search."

"That's two days away!" Joe cried. "Anything could happen to her in that time!"

"I know," William said, "but we can't help it. Come on, let's go eat supper."

"Wait," Joe said, remembering the bundle he had left in the shed. "Here, Dad, I forgot to tell you about this." He handed the sweater-wrapped package to his father and told how he had discovered it in the cave.

"Well, let's go take a look at what old High Elk hid away," said William, leading the way to the house.

Inside, Marie, who had bathed and put on clean jeans, was setting the table. Grandma was peeling potatoes and when she saw Joe she immediately started to scold.

"Has my grandson told you of his foolishness?" she said in Lakota. "He took the little girl and the filly and exposed them to the dangers of the storm. The horse is lost. *Oh hinh,*" she wailed. "The pony will be eaten by the wild dogs. We should have sold her to the white man who wanted her when she was born!"

"*Ina,*" William replied in Lakota. "The boy has told of his foolishness. Do not scold, he has sorrow for what has happened."

"And he should," Grandma continued, ignoring her son. "My granddaughter comes home with mud on her good school dress and see," she pointed to Joe's muddy jeans, "his good pants are ruined also. They will have to wear rags to school tomorrow, for the clothes cannot be washed and dried until the morning."

"The mud will wash out," Joe's mother said, coming into the kitchen. She had changed her white uniform to slacks and an old blouse.

"The boy was at least wise enough to take shelter so that he and Marie were safe from the storm. They also removed their shoes before walking in the mud."

Grandma disgustedly turned her back to the family. She thought her daughter-in-law was too lenient with the children.

"But, Joe," asked his mother, "where is Marie's sweater?"

"Here, Marlene," said William. "Move the dishes over for a while, Marie, so that we can see what old High Elk's treasure is."

Marie had told Marlene and Grandma about Joe's finding the leather-wrapped bundle and they came closer to see, but Grandma hung back a little.

"*Teḣinda,* forbidden," the old woman said. She still believed many of the old superstitions. "Careful," she warned, "there may be a *wanaǵi,* ghost, in it." But she moved a little nearer.

"Do you know of this?" William asked his mother as he began to remove Marie's sweater.

Hands to her face, ready to shut out the sight of a ghost if one appeared, Grandma nodded. "My husband's grandfather told of how he had hidden a story thing in the cave. He warned of not disturbing it until a hundred years had passed."

"A hundred years," mused her son. "Why it must be nearly that now. Did he say the year he had hidden it?"

"No, he had no use for the year's number. It must have been after he moved into the cave."

"Let's see. We're pretty sure that he came to the reservation about

1876, for didn't he tell that it was the time of the barren autumn after the Little Big Horn?"

"Yes," said Grandma, lowering her eyes, "he knew of that battle."

"He didn't fight Custer, did he, Grandma?" excitedly asked Joe.

Grandma covered her mouth with her hands, her eyes became blank and she mumbled, "We must not speak for a hundred years."

William looked at his mother in surprise. His mind was busy with speculations about what was in the package he was unwrapping, but he suddenly comprehended what his mother had said. He took his hands from the bundle which, free of the sweater, lay in what only seemed to be a rotten roll of rawhide. He gazed into his mother's eyes as if trying to force her to say more, but she looked away and shook her head.

Joe sensed the tension between them. "What is it? What's the matter?" he cried.

William still stood, quietly staring at his mother, then he looked at Joe as he decided what to do.

"Years ago," he explained, "almost one hundred years ago, a large gathering of the Sioux and Cheyenne defeated General Custer at the Battle of the Little Big Horn."

"I know that," Joe said, wanting to forestall a history lesson and get back to whatever was wrapped in the rawhide.

William held up his hand to signify patience. "The soldiers who came to punish the Indians after the battle wanted very much to know who killed Custer. The warriors, who were in the battle and who knew which brave killed the general, vowed not to speak of it again for a hundred years."

Joe was awed. "Do you think it was Grandpa?"

"*Hinh, hinh,*" wailed Grandma. "Do not say such a thing. We will be punished!"

"Do not worry, *Ina,*" William comforted. "Whatever High Elk hid in here," he reverently put his hand on the bundle, "will not bring punishment on us. Those bad days are gone. It may," he went on, thinking aloud, "bring us good instead."

"Aren't you going to open it now, Dad?" Joe asked hopefully, already sensing that his father was holding back for some reason.

"Not yet. I think it is important that when we do open it, we do so in the presence of someone whose word will not be doubted."

"What do you mean?" Joe asked.

"Too often in the past our people have lost valuable tribal treasures.

Whatever is in here," William said, placing his hand on the bundle, "may be valuable historically, as well as being worth money. We don't want to lose it."

"I don't understand," said Joe.

"You must remember that when the Indians were first confined to reservations they were at the mercy of the soldiers. The government wanted to wipe out the people's old way of life, and as the bands came to the reservation all of their possessions, which they valued as a free people, were taken from them. Not only weapons, but pipes, medicine bags, *parfleches,* ceremonial robes—anything that would be a reminder of their past culture—were put in a pile and burned. The Indians became sly and lied about their belongings and hid them, as High Elk probably hid this."

"That is true," said Grandma. "If a person saved something of the past it was taken from him. But not everything was burned. There were white people who took many things for their own."

William nodded his head in agreement. "Yes, they did," he went on. "And the people caught on to the white man's desire to own old things, and because they were a poor, starving people, they began to sell what little they had left. Some also learned that an article was worth more if it were thought to be very old, or if it had belonged to some famous Indian, like Crazy Horse. So some began to make things and claim that what they made had belonged to a great-grandfather, or to a well-known chief. This happened often enough to cause white people to be distrustful of any new discovery until it was checked by an expert."

"Gee," said Joe, "we'll have to be sure that everyone believes what I found is the real thing."

"That's right," William answered. "But today there are false white men who pose as experts and take a treasure from an innocent Indian, promising to prove its history. They are thieves, because they never return the article. So when we open the bundle we must do so in the presence of someone who knows about historical items, but we must make sure that he is also an honest man."

"What are you going to do?" asked Joe.

"Tomorrow I'll go to the tribal office and tell the council of your discovery. They'll want to know what is in the bundle and they should know an expert to contact to be here when we open it.

"But first," William continued, going to an old trunk where the family kept some things that had belonged to High Elk, "we will wrap it in High Elk's buffalo robe." He took out an old tanned hide which showed much wear, but was still intact.

"We will give it to Grandma to keep and guard," he said, handing the bundle to his mother, "for she is always at home to see that it is safe."

The old woman held it in her arms, still fearful of the wanáǵi. Then she carried it to her room.

Wild Horse Catchers!

AS HE WAS EATING breakfast the next morning Joe worked out a plan to drop Marie at school and then to go on to the wildlife preserve and search for Star, even though he would have to do it on foot because he couldn't risk riding the pregnant Śungwiye. But his father forestalled any such notion.

"We'll give you a ride to school today, Joe," William said.

"You don't have to do that," protested Joe. "We can walk. The water in the creek must be low enough to cross. Besides, you might be late for work."

"No, Joe," his mother said, "the creek and the path will be too muddy and you and Marie will be all dirty by the time you get to school."

"Don't worry about us, Joe," William added. "I want to stop at your school anyway so I can use Mr. Gray Bear's phone to call the ranger. Otherwise, I would have to wait until noon to call from work."

They arrived at school a whole hour earlier than they usually did. William went to the principal's house to explain their early arrival. Mrs. Gray Bear insisted that the children wait in the house after their parents left.

"I'm sorry about Star, Joe," Mr. Gray Bear said. "But I'm glad you're here early. You can help me and the janitor clean up the school yard."

Broken branches and other debris left by the storm were strewn all over the playground and Joe kept busy until classes started. In the classroom his thoughts wandered from the subject he was supposed to be studying to worrying about Star and wondering what the bundle contained. He was glad that Mr. Gray Bear didn't call on him to answer any questions.

Finally the agonizingly slow school day ended and as Joe waited for Marie he talked with Mr. Blue Shield, the High Elks' neighbor, who had come to pick up his children.

"Say, Joe," Mr. Blue Shield said, "have you folks lost your filly?"

"Yes, yesterday in the storm," Joe said, unhappily.

"Well, I think I saw her this afternoon."

"Where?" eagerly asked Joe.

"Well, I'm not sure it was your horse. Does she have a lame leg?"

Joe nodded and the man went on. "I was looking for strays that got away yesterday and I rode up on top of Bald Peak to get a good view of the land; you know you can see pretty far from up there."

"Yes," Joe agreed, wishing Mr. Blue Shield would hurry and tell about Star.

"I was looking east and south over your range when I saw a horse coming out of the trees by the creek. I have some new field glasses so that I can see real good for miles. Anyway, I looked and I'll be darned if it didn't look like your filly. The critter had the same star blaze on her forehead and white stockings like your filly. She was limping pretty bad."

"She wasn't cut up or anything, was she?" Joe asked.

"No, just seemed to be favoring her right hind leg."

"Gee, thanks Mr. Blue Shield. I'm going right over to have a look in that area." He started off and then remembered that the place where Mr. Blue Shield had seen Star was about ten miles from home, and he had no horse.

"Guess I can't go," he said to Mr. Blue Shield. "Śungwiye is too close to foaling to ride."

"Well, now, maybe I can help you out," Mr. Blue Shield said. "I came over with the jeep since I was looking for strays along the way. I'll get my kids and we'll drop Marie home. Then you and I can cut across your range. I'll take you south of the Bald where I think your filly is."

"Thanks, Mr. Blue Shield. I'd sure appreciate it if you would. I hate to lose any more time looking for Star."

Joe rode up in front of the jeep with Mr. Blue Shield, while Marie and the two Blue Shield girls rode in the back. The girls, all about the same age, squealed with delight as they bounced over the rough path to the High Elks'. The creek was low, although still muddy, but the four-wheel drive vehicle had no difficulty getting through.

At the High Elks' house Joe ran to the horse shed to get a rope halter and Marie reluctantly got out of the jeep with instructions to tell Grandma where Joe was going.

"Can't I come, Joe?" Marie begged.

"No, I'll have to move quickly if I want to catch Star and get home before dark," Joe answered. "You stay here with Grandma."

"But they get to go," Marie said, pointing to the Blue Shield girls still in the jeep.

"They're not going to hunt for Star," said Mr. Blue Shield. "I'm going to take them home after I let Joe off."

The Blue Shields' small cattle ranch was on the west of the High Elk range. They had a new house, identical to the one Joe's family lived in, built in the western foothills of the Lodge Pole Ridge. It was a lovely home site, sheltered from the prevailing northwest winter winds. The only problem was that the water for cattle was in a creek on the east side. Many years ago the Blue Shields had made arrangements with the High Elks to cross the cattle over their range to water. The two families were good friends as well as neighbors and the trail between their homes, which crossed above the Bald Peak, was well traveled by horse, and in recent years by the Blue Shields' jeep.

As the jeep bumped over the open plains into the foothills of the ridge, Joe scanned the horizon with Mr. Blue Shield's field glasses, looking for Star.

"That filly of yours must be a pretty smart horse," said Mr. Blue Shield. "She must have known that if she crossed the creek she'd be on home ground. Something must have frightened her or I'm sure she would have headed for home."

"Did you see which way she went?" asked Joe.

"It looked to me like she was heading toward the south ridge. She must be about ten to twelve miles from home."

"I think I'll climb up on the Bald to see if I can spot her before I start searching along the south ridge," Joe planned.

"Good idea," agreed Mr. Blue Shield. "Why don't you use my glasses, you'll be able to see everywhere with them."

"Thanks, I will."

"You can borrow one of my horses, too, if you want," the neighbor offered.

"No, I'd better not. I'd sure hate to lose one of your horses too, Mr. Blue Shield, and besides if I see Star and she's close enough to hear my whistle, she'll come."

"Okay, but if you change your mind you can sure use one. Tell you what," Mr. Blue Shield went on, "I'll take the kids on home and then in an hour or so I'll come on back to take you home. No, no," he said as Joe started to protest, "that's okay. I still have some stray stock out and I can look for them at the same time. Besides, you'd never be able to hike the ten miles home before dark. I'll meet you at the base of the Bald."

Joe got out of the jeep on the south side of the Bald Peak where the narrow trail began its steep spiral upwards. He was grateful to Mr. Blue Shield but he was vexed with himself. "I'm a stupid jerk for not thinking about how to get home." He guessed he'd planned to ride Star, forgetting about her lame leg. "Joe, you're absolutely brainless," he said out loud to the hills.

He swiftly began the climb to the top of the peak. Its base was similar to the rest of the ridge, thickly wooded with brush and the tall, straight pines for which the ridge was named. The nomadic Sioux had found the lightweight but strong trees ideal supports for their skin lodges. About three-quarters of the way to the summit the greenery stopped and the peak jutted out over the open prairie, providing an unhampered view.

As he climbed, Joe thought of the legends of how this one peak became so bare. One story told of two monstrous bears who waged a gigantic battle to the death, uprooting trees and tearing giant boulders out of the ground. Another tale, and Joe's favorite, was of two great stallions who fought over the right to the herd of wild horses below.

Joe always vividly imagined the fury of such a fight as he recalled the story. The old king, leader of the herd for many years, accepted the challenge of a younger male who had been previously driven from the herd. Joe could almost hear them squeal with foaming mouths, as they reared and lunged at each other. They beat with quick kicking forehooves and deadly slashing rear ones. The maddened animals bit and ripped until both were smeared with their mingled blood. Whirling, they charged and the force of the impact hurled both to the ground. Nothing impeded their struggle. The slender pines received the brunt of the crashing falls until, uprooted, they toppled. Dirt and rocks flew under the stallions' sharp, scrambling hooves. At last the aged king's strength gave way to the challenger's youthful energy and speed, but he would not run. The old one fought until after one last, desperate charge, weakened by great exertion and loss of blood, he fell and could not rise. Joe would tremble as he visualized the victor striking, with rapid hooves, the final mortal blow. The new monarch turned, and stood triumphant on the rim of the precipice, trumpeting his victory to the herd below.

The legend was still vivid in his mind as Joe quickly climbed the narrow trail which zigzagged through the pines and onto the bare crest. On top he held the glasses to his eyes and scanned the semicircle before him.

Fascinated by the sudden nearness of the cars on the highway, he slowly swept the strong lenses toward his house where he could see Šungwiye contentedly browsing in the corral. The trees along the creek, the school and the wildlife preserve all seemed within touching distance. As he shifted the glasses to the south of the creek he saw from the quickened sway of the tree tops that the mustang herd was crossing.

The lead mare, emerging on the near side, paused, surveyed the open plain and galloped on, the herd following. The scrawny, wiry horses, an occasional domesticated breed among them, swept through the grass into the shelter of the southern ridge. Something had fright-ened them into leaving the protection of the preserve.

Joe moved the glasses back to the spot where the horses had come out from the trees. Two riders came galloping out of the woods and then stopped. Instinctively Joe ducked, although the men could not see him. Stretching full length on the flat rock, he held the men in sight. They seemed to be arguing about whether to follow the herd. One pointed to the way they had come, the other to the ridge ahead. Joe quickly lowered his head as he saw one man aim a pair of glasses at the ridge.

They were horse catchers, Joe knew, hunting the wild herd ille-gally on the preserve. The men may have deliberately stampeded the horses onto the open range where, if the men were Indian and could hunt on reservation land, the wild mustangs would be fair game. From this distance Joe couldn't tell. Their faces, in the shadow of the wide brim of their cowboy hats, were dark, but men who lived much in the out-of-doors all had sunburned skins.

No matter if they were Indian or white, they were daring enough to break the law and, therefore, dangerous. Joe's heart was pumping madly as he thought of his lost filly. Unbranded, she would be a prime catch for lawless men.

He cautiously raised his head, but with his naked eye could not see the men. He eased the glasses up and searched. He could not spot them. It was then that he saw Star.

The filly was quite near, partially concealed in the brush of the hillock of the lower ridge to the south. She was still, staring down toward the Bald trail. Joe raised himself until he could see down the side of the ridge and spotted the horse catchers riding up. Frantic, he knew that on the next turn they would see Star. He jumped to his feet and slipped off his shirt. Yelling at the top of his lungs like a charging wild cat, he whirled the shirt over his head. Frightened, the filly snorted and turned into the sheltering brush and pines, but the men saw Joe.

The Rescue

JOE DUCKED DOWN among the boulders and wondered what to do. He could hear the curses of the men as they fought to get their startled horses under control.

"There's a kid up there!" one of them yelled. "He's seen us, we'd better get him!"

Joe jumped over the rocks and dead branches, running to the more difficult path down the north side of the Bald Peak. He had often climbed this faint trail looking for agates and arrowheads and he knew that men on horses could not follow him. It was almost straight down. Most of the way he slid on the seat of his pants, digging the heels of his boots into the ground to slow the painful ride. Pants torn, boots badly scuffed, and with many scratches from the whipping pine branches, he landed at the bottom of the ridge. Looking up, he could not see the men, but realized they would know from the noise of his descent which way he had gone. Fearing that one of the men would use the rifle he had on his saddle, Joe traveled through the concealing brush at the base of the peak and hurried toward the road to the Blue Shields'. He had to find Mr. Blue Shield before the horse catchers could ride down the south trail.

He ran up the rough road and heard the motor of the jeep as it topped the rise of the ridge. Waving his arms, Joe brought Mr. Blue Shield to a brake-slamming halt.

"There are horse catchers coming down the south trail," he panted, jumping into the jeep. "And I saw Star."

"Boy, you look like you've tangled with a wildcat," exclaimed Mr. Blue Shield.

"I had to get down the north side pretty fast," Joe explained. "Those men must know I saw them chasing the mustangs out of the preserve. I scared Star away so that they wouldn't see her, but they started after me—so I lit out down this side. I'm afraid they'll find Star," he stopped, out of breath.

"Well, now," said Mr. Blue Shield, "we'd better get out of here." He turned the jeep around on the rough road.

"What are we going to do?" asked Joe.

"We're going to my place to get a couple of horses for us to ride so that we can get that filly before those horse catchers do. This old jeep can go about anyplace, but not up the Bald. I'll send my wife and kids over to your place for your dad."

"Dad won't be home until six," said Joe.

Mr. Blue Shield checked his watch. "It's almost five thirty now, by the time my wife gets there he ought to be pulling in. Let's hope he's not late. We might need his help."

Joe pulled his shirt on over his scratched and skinned back, as they drove into the Blue Shields' yard.

"You start saddling up the horses," directed Mr. Blue Shield, "while I tell the wife."

Joe ran into the corral and caught the bay mare he knew Mr. Blue Shield always rode. By the time he had finished saddling and bridling her, Mr. Blue Shield had caught another horse.

"I'd better ride bareback, Mr. Blue Shield," Joe said, handing over the reins of the horse he'd saddled. "I'm not used to a saddle."

"Okay, Joe, jump on then. These ponies are used to bareback riders. My girls ride that way all of the time," Mr. Blue Shield said as he mounted.

Mrs. Blue Shield and the girls, their eyes round with excitement, were driving up the road as the man and boy rode out of the yard.

"We'll let them go on before us," Mr. Blue Shield said. "The sound of the jeep's motor might scare those horse catchers into being cautious."

"Gosh, I hope they haven't found Star," Joe said.

"I don't think they have yet. It'll take them a while to get down the south trail and around to the north side to see where you went."

"What will we do if we see them?" Joe asked nervously.

"That depends on what *they* do," answered Mr. Blue Shield.

As they rode down to the base of the Bald they saw the jeep bouncing over the range toward the High Elks'.

"We'll act like we're looking for strays," instructed Mr. Blue Shield.

They scanned the ridge as they walked the horses around to the north side. Mr. Blue Shield used his field glasses to get a better view. As they rode near the bottom of the trail, Joe saw the horse catchers.

"There they are," he said softly, "and they've got Star."

Mr. Blue Shield made no comment, but continued riding up to the men.

The horse catchers had lassoed the filly. One of the men was mounted. He was backing his horse, attempting to keep the rope taut around Star's neck. The other man, on foot, was vainly trying to slip a halter over the head of the struggling horse. Star's ears were flat and she was snorting and snapping at the man on the ground as she whirled closer to slash her hind hooves at the mounted horse. The men were yelling and clearly having a difficult time. They didn't hear the approach of the man and boy.

"I see you found one of the strays we've been looking for," said Mr. Blue Shield calmly.

The men ceased struggling with Star. The rope hung loosely from her neck and from the mounted man's saddle. The filly lowered her head and began browsing unconcernedly.

"Whatta you mean, your stray?" the mounted man asked belligerently. "This ain't no tame horse, she's as wild as any mustang."

"She's mine," said Joe.

The man looked closely at Joe, recognizing him as the boy who had startled his horse. "Say, you're the kid who spooked our horses. Now what did you do that for?"

"I didn't want you to get my horse," answered Joe, pointing to Star.

The man looked at Star and said, "You can't prove she's yours, she ain't branded."

Joe glared helplessly at the mean-looking white man, but before Joe could answer him Mr. Blue Shield said, "You men must be new around here, not to know a High Elk horse." He was staring at the younger man who stood nervously coiling the halter rope. As Mr. Blue Shield spoke the young man looked up and they saw that he was an Indian, not too much older than Joe.

"Are you High Elk?" the strange young Indian asked Mr. Blue Shield.

"I am," answered Joe.

"You?" The young man looked startled.

"Joe High Elk," Joe explained. "My dad is William and we own this filly."

"I still say you can't prove it," said the white man. "If she's a tame horse, how come she put up such a fight when I tried to halter her?"

"She's been ridden only by High Elks and handled only by High Elks since she was born. Maybe she doesn't like your smell!" Joe retorted, urging the horse he was riding nearer to Star, who now stood nervously watching Joe.

The white man was angry. "You're a pretty mouthy kid, ain't you?" he said, barring Joe's approach to Star. "I say the filly's wild and claim her 'cause we caught her." He motioned to the man on the ground to grab hold of the dangling rope.

"I'll prove she's mine," Joe said, dismounting. "I can walk right up to her and she'll let me mount her, even without a halter!"

"Wait!" ordered the white man to his partner. "Hang on to that rope."

But the young Indian dropped the rope. "Let the kid try," he said.

Joe walked slowly to Star. He hoped that all the excitement she'd been through wouldn't have made her wary of everyone.

"Easy, Star. Good girl," he said in a quiet, reassuring tone.

The filly stood still as he approached, ears perked forward at his voice. She gave a small nicker as his hand went to her face.

"How are you, girl?" Joe went on in the same gentle tone, all the while patting and stroking the filly's back as he eased his way to her side. She trembled as he grabbed a hand hold in her mane to swing himself up to her back, but she let him mount.

"Good girl," Joe said thankfully. He had never before mounted Star without a bridle or halter to control her. He felt lucky that she'd permitted it now. He loosened the lasso and slid it over her head. Star shook her head as the rope fell, glad to be free of its restraint.

"Guess that proves it," said Mr. Blue Shield. "I think you guys better get out of here. You're on private land."

Thwarted, the white man angrily coiled the lasso to his saddle horn. "Come on," he said to his partner, and rode off.

The young Indian climbed onto his horse, which he had tied to a nearby bush. He hesitated as if to say something, changed his mind and cantered after the white man.

"Better stay out of the preserve too," warned Mr. Blue Shield.

Joe eased himself off the filly, fearful that any abrupt movement would startle her into running off again. Keeping a hand in her mane, he slipped the halter over her head and started leading her home.

As Joe and Mr. Blue Shield headed for the High Elk home, they heard the motor of the jeep and saw it speeding toward them.

"That must be your dad," said Mr. Blue Shield. "My wife's too scared to drive that fast."

"You've found Star," said William as he braked the jeep. "Where? And where are the horse catchers?"

"Hold on," said Mr. Blue Shield dismounting, "you ride home with Joe and he'll tell you all about it. I'll take the jeep to collect my family."

"Well, Joe," said the boy's father. "Seems like you have another story to tell me."

Howard High Elk

THE BLUE SHIELDS STAYED for supper with the High Elks at Marlene's insistence. As they ate, Joe and Mr. Blue Shield told the details of their encounter with the horse catchers.

"Did you recognize the men?" asked William.

"No," answered Mr. Blue Shield, "I never saw either of them before. But, you know, there was a young Indian with them and he reminded me of someone, but I can't think of who it could be."

The two men and Joe went out to the horse shed to check on Śungwiye and Star while the women cleaned up after supper. Marie, who seldom had company, was happily playing with the Blue Shield girls.

"Looks like the filly is glad to be home," said Mr. Blue Shield as he watched Star contentedly munching hay.

William nodded. "She's lucky that her leg isn't too badly hurt." He had examined it earlier and found the injury to be only a sprain, which he had firmly bandaged to give support as it healed.

"You kids will have to walk to school for several weeks," he said to Joe.

Joe nodded. That wouldn't be so bad, as there were only a few weeks of school left.

"You can ride my horses tomorrow," kindly offered Mr. Blue Shield.

"Thanks," said William. "Leave both horses here and Joe can return them to your place after school."

"Your mare's due soon, isn't she?" asked their neighbor.

"Should be any day now," replied William. "Joe, here, has been babying her so that she ought to give a healthy foal."

"I hope she gives you a stud colt," Mr. Blue Shield said, knowing of their dreams. "My father had one of your horses and it was the best all-around ranch horse we ever had. There should be more of them. Well," he turned toward the house, "I better round up my family. I have a few chores to do before dark."

"Thank you for your help, Albert. I'm glad we got Star back. Joe couldn't have done it alone."

"That's okay, Will," his friend answered. "You've helped me out many times in the past. Guess that's what neighbors are for."

"Thank you, Mr. Blue Shield," said Joe. "Dad's right, I couldn't have caught Star alone. When she's well I'd sure be glad to lend you a hand on your ranch this summer." He wanted to do something for the man who had done so much for him.

"Say, Joe, I just might take you up on that offer. My girls don't make very good cowboys and there are times when I could use another hand."

The three girls protested at not being able to play longer, but Mrs. Blue Shield invited Marie to come to their house soon and Marlene promised that she could.

Joe and his father stood watching their neighbors ride off in their jeep. "That's a good man to have for a friend and neighbor," William said. "I'm glad you offered to help him, Joe. Now don't take any money if he offers it."

"Oh, I won't, Dad," and then remembering the bundle he said, "Did you talk to anyone about the thing I found in the cave?"

"Yes, I did," his father said. "I called the tribal chairman, Frank Iron Cloud. He agreed with me that we should have an expert on hand when we open the bundle. He suggested I call Dr. Scott—you remember, he's one of the men from the university who was out here last summer. He and Frank will drive out here tomorrow."

"What did Dr. Scott say?" asked Joe.

"He sounded pretty excited over the phone. He was pleased that I had called him to be an 'authoritative witness,' as he put it."

"What do you think it is, Dad?"

"I don't even want to guess. It might be of value and then it could be just an old rolled-up strip of rawhide. We'll have to wait and see."

Musing over the possibilities of what the bundle might contain, they started toward the house.

"Hey, what's that?" Joe said, hearing a noise. "Listen, I thought I heard a horse."

"Well, we have four of them here," his father said. "Quite a herd for a change."

"No," Joe insisted. "What I heard seemed to be coming from the creek."

They stood, straining their ears to the early evening's unbroken quiet. Suddenly they heard the neigh of a horse, closer this time, and one of the Blue Shield horses whinnied in reply.

"You're right, Joe. There's a rider coming up the path from the creek."

They waited and as the mounted figure came nearer, Joe recognized him as the young Indian he'd seen with Star. "It's one of the horse catchers!"

William walked toward the approaching horse. "What do you want?" he demanded.

The young man reined in by the corral. "Are you High Elk?" he asked.

"Yes, I am. What do you want?" Joe's father asked.

"Don't want to cause any trouble, I've had enough. . . ." The strange Indian's voice faded as he swayed in the saddle.

Quickly William was at the horse's side, "You're hurt. Here Joe, take care of his horse. I'll help him into the house."

"But, Dad," Joe protested, "he's one of the men who tried to steal Star!"

"Never mind, Joe. This boy is hurt and we'll help him." William assisted the young man down and supported him to the house.

Puzzled as to why the young Indian would come to the High Elks' home, Joe quickly unsaddled the horse, slipped its bridle, turned it into the corral with the Blue Shield horses and ran into the house.

William had put the young man on the bed in the living room and was pulling the boy's soiled boots off.

"I'm okay. I can sit up, I don't want to be a bother," the stranger protested.

"But your face," said Marlene.

Joe walked closer and saw the young man's face was bruised and battered, one eye was swollen shut and dried blood covered a cut on his cheek.

The young Indian lifted a hand to his apparently painful eye. "Yeah, I bet I really look rough. Martin sort of knocked me around."

"Martin?" asked William. "Is that the white man you were with?"

The boy nodded. "He didn't like it much when I let you mount your horse," he said to Joe. "Then when I told him I was splitting, he really got mad." He sat up holding his head.

"Marlene," William said, "fix him something to eat. Come," he said to the boy, "let's get you cleaned up and see how badly you've been hurt. Then you can tell us about it."

Later, his face cleansed and a Band-Aid over the cut, the young man sat at the table eating hungrily.

"Now, first off," William asked, "who are you?"

"My name is Howard Anderson since my step-father adopted me, but my real last name is Pretty Flute."

"Pretty Flute?" mused William. "There used to be a family of that name on this reservation."

The boy nodded, "Yes, my dad was born at the agency, but moved to Los Angeles after the Second World War." He paused and looked at William. "My mother's maiden name was Irene High Elk. Her father was Howard High Elk."

The family was quiet, surprised at the boy's identity. Grandma's keening wail broke the silence.

"*Oh hinh.* I know of this Irene. She once wrote a letter to my husband. Her man had died and she needed money to raise her young son. But we had bad times and had nothing to send. My husband was sad about not being able to help his niece. We always wondered what happened to her and the boy."

"Can you tell us whatever happened to your grandfather, Howard High Elk? We have never known where he went after he sold the land and horses." William explained.

"Yes, I can," Howard answered. "Grandpa told me everything about himself. He moved somewhere in Nebraska and lived there until all of his money was gone. His daughter was born there, but when she was a baby the family moved near Beulah, Wyoming. Howard worked for a rancher there. He always loved horses and in the last years of his life he regretted leaving this place. He always wanted to bring Irene here to visit, but was not sure of the welcome he would get. I don't know how my mother met my father, but it was during the war, and after it was over they moved to California.

"Grandpa got too old to work, and he was so lonely after Grandma died that he moved to live with us in California. I remember him very well because after my father died, I used to stay home with Grandpa while Mom worked. He used to talk about the famous High Elk herd and how he always wished he could see it again. He told me the story of High Elk's cave, and the stallion legend of Bald Peak."

Howard paused to take a drink of water, then continued.

"After he died my mother got married again to a white man, George Anderson. He was okay. He was good to me and we got along all right, but then he moved us to Wyoming. He had worked for the Bureau of Indian Affairs Employment Service in Los Angeles and that's where my mother met him when she went there to get help in finding a job. Well, he was tired of the city and transferred to Wyoming. I was sort of excited about moving. My step-dad said I could have a horse, which I always wanted, because of Grandpa's stories I suppose.

"At first it was fine when we moved last summer. I got my horse, learned to ride and really liked the mountains where we lived, but then school started."

Again he paused, as if wondering how to tell the rest.

"You know, I never thought much about being an Indian. I knew I was, but didn't think that made me different from anyone else. Where I went to school in L. A. there were all kinds of people: blacks, Japanese, whites, Chicanos and a few Indians. We got along okay. But in the new school, I didn't know what I was. The white kids called me an Indian, like it was a dirty word; the Indian kids called me a white man because of my step-dad. I didn't have any friends. I got into fights and started skipping school—I hated the place! Then I was suspended. My mom cried. My step-dad got mad. They didn't know what to do with me. I knew I was a big problem, so I split."

"Split?" asked William, puzzled at the term.

"You know, Dad," said Joe. "He left. Ran away."

"Right," Howard continued. "I really didn't know where I was going, but I bummed in this direction."

"You hitchhiked?" asked Joe.

"Yes. When I got to the town north of this reservation I knew I had to come here, but wasn't sure how. I got a job at a gas station there and then met Martin, who used to hang around the place. When he found out I could ride he asked me if I wanted a job rounding up wild horses. I didn't know anything about wild horses, except for what Grandpa used to tell and I thought it would be a great job and a chance to get down here. I honestly didn't know," he said to William, "that we would be hunting on a protected preserve or that I was even anyplace near the High Elk land.

"Martin had a cattle truck that we came down in with two horses in the back. He said I could have one of the horses to keep for helping him. He also said he'd pay me half the money after he sold the wild horses we caught. It sounded like a good deal. But now I know that Martin is a crook and probably wouldn't have paid me anything.

"When I found out where I was, and who you were," he said to Joe, "and that we were trying to steal a High Elk horse, I was just sick.

"Man, I wanted to get away from that Martin, but I was afraid of him. He chewed me out good for letting you get the filly and I told him I was through. That's when he hit me. He knocked me down, jumped on his horse and left me by the creek. Why he didn't take my horse, I don't know."

"The horse was probably stolen," said William. "Boy, you've had quite a time. How old are you?"

"Almost eighteen. I would have graduated from high school this year if I'd stayed in school," Howard said sadly.

"I bet your mother is worried sick about you," said Marlene. "We'll have to let her know you're here."

"Yes," said William, "we'll do that tomorrow, but for now you can bed down in Joe's room. No," he said as Howard started to protest, "you're our boy, just as if you had always lived here. We Indians take care of our own."

Joe and Howard

THE DAY IN SCHOOL PASSED even more slowly than the previous one had. The excitement of Star's rescue and of having a member of the long-lost Howard High Elk family appear and then to have this relative turn out to be one of the horse catchers was almost too much for Joe to comprehend. Most exciting of all would be this evening's visit from Frank Iron Cloud and Dr. Scott. Would they finally get to open the mysterious bundle? Joe couldn't even begin to concentrate on his studies with such things on his mind.

At last, he was able to pick up Marie and head for home. They were riding one of the Blue Shield's horses which was older and slower than Star. Joe couldn't even kick her into a trot and it seemed forever before they got home.

Howard was waiting by the corral as they rode into the yard. He had his horse saddled and the other Blue Shield horse ready to go.

"Hi," he greeted Joe and Marie. "I'll ride over to the Blue Shields with you, Joe, so that you won't have to walk back."

"Has Śungwiye had her baby yet?" asked Marie, running into the shed to see for herself.

"Not a baby," corrected Joe. "That's what people have. Horses have foals." He followed her into the shed.

"Well, it'll still be a baby," said Marie.

"The mare acts sort of restless," Howard said. "She's been nipping at Star and wouldn't let me touch her when I went in to water her."

"She doesn't know you yet, Howard," said Marie.

The boys looked at each other and laughed, both remembering Star's aversion to strangers yesterday.

Śungwiye was now standing calmly in her stall. She nickered softly at Joe as he walked in beside her, gently running his hand over her neck. Star also gave greeting, wanting her share of attention, but the mare laid her ears back and reached her head over the stall's partition to nip at the filly.

"What's the matter, Šungwiye?" crooned Joe. "Is it getting about time for that foal to come?" The mare tossed her head as if she agreed with him.

Joe walked into Star's stall, "Come on, Star, we better get you out of the maternity ward. Šungwiye doesn't want you around." He led the filly into the corral and saw that she was still favoring her bandaged leg. "You'll be okay out here. We're taking the other horses home."

Grandma came to the corral as Joe led Star out of the shed.

"That is a good idea," she said, "to let the mare be alone in her stall."

"Do you think she'll be all right while we take the Blue Shield horses home?" asked Joe.

Grandma gave a little laugh, "There is nothing you can do. Šungwiye is a wise old mother, she will not need help and it will be a while before it happens."

"Well, we'll hurry back," Joe said and then it occurred to him that Grandma had been speaking English. As they rode off, leading the horse, he teased her in Lakota, "Hey, *Unci, wašicun niye un?*"

"Humph," Grandma grumbled and then commanded, "*Iyopte!*"

Joe rode off laughing.

"What was that all about?" asked Howard, who hadn't understood a word.

"I'm sorry, Howard," Joe said, still laughing. "I guess I'm not as polite as Grandma. She so seldom speaks English that I forget that she can. She was being considerate of you because she knew you can't understand Lakota. I had to tease her a little bit and I asked her if she was a white woman now and she got disgusted with me and said to 'Get going!'"

The boys laughed. "I'd like to learn how to talk Indian," Howard said. "Why do you call the language 'Lakota' instead of Sioux?"

"It's complicated and I'm not sure I really understand why," Joe said, "but I'll try to explain.

"The Sioux have different ways of pronouncing the same word. I think it is called an accent. No," pondered Joe, "that's not right."

"Do you mean 'dialect?'" Howard suggested.

"Yes, that's the word. Dialect. Some of the Sioux used the 'd' in their dialect and others used the 'l' so that 'Dakota' became 'Lakota' even though they were the same word. In the Lakota dialect all words with a 'd' sound are replaced by the 'l' sound. The word 'thank you,' for example, is '*pidamiye*' in Dakota. The Lakota change it to '*pilamiye*.'"

"Wow," exclaimed Howard. "That sounds difficult. I don't think I'll ever be able to learn to speak Sioux—I mean Lakota."

"It's not hard," protested Joe. "If you are around here very long you'll have to learn. Grandma will get tired of talking English and then we'll all have to speak Lakota to her."

"I guess my family lived with white people too long, because we speak only English at home." Thinking of his home, Howard added, "I talked to my mother on the telephone this morning."

William had taken Howard into the agency with him this morning to make the call.

"What did she say?" asked Joe.

"She was glad to hear my voice and happy to know where I was. I talked to my step-dad too. I was afraid that he would be angry, but he apologized to me. He blamed himself for my running away because he'd been so mad at me before."

"Are they coming after you?"

"Not for two weeks. They can't get away from work until then, but your father said I could stay here and maybe help Mr. Blue Shield out. I guess your neighbor will be busy with cows calving and can use help."

"I'm glad you can stay for a while longer," Joe said happily. "I can show you all around the High Elk range. What about your horse?" he asked, referring to the animal which they thought Martin had stolen.

"Your father reported Martin to the police and also told them about the horse. They'll keep an eye out for reports of a stolen horse, but said I might as well keep her out here until they hear something. The police said the chances of finding out who the horse belonged to were slim, because Martin has a suspicious record of all kinds of illegal activities, such as rustling, as well as capturing wild horses. Man, am I glad I got away from him before I really got into trouble."

When the boys arrived at the neighboring ranch, Mr. Blue Shield was surprised, but pleased, at Howard's identity. "I thought you reminded me of someone," he said. "I knew your father, and you resemble him."

"I'm going to be around for the next two weeks, Mr. Blue Shield," Howard said. "I'd be willing to work for you if you can use me."

"Yes, I sure can use some help now," Mr. Blue Shield said accepting Howard's offer. "Even if my girls were old enough to lend a hand, I couldn't take them out of school. I'd be glad to pay you," he offered.

"No, sir," refused Howard. "I want to do it for nothing. Besides I'm green at ranch work and might not be as much help as you'd like."

The boys refused Mrs. Blue Shield's invitation to lunch, explaining that Śungwiye might be going into labor. They rode off in high spirits.

"Man, this is an uncomfortable ride," complained Joe, who was sitting in back of Howard.

"The saddle seat is more comfortable," laughed Howard. "Why do you always ride bareback?"

"We only have one saddle," Joe explained, "and we save that for special occasions because we couldn't afford a new one if that wore out. Anyway, Dad also says that it's safer riding bareback because Marie and I ride double to school. At least, there is no danger of being hung up in a stirrup if we ever get thrown."

The boys, in spite of their age difference, were enjoying each other's company. Howard listened sympathetically to Joe's story of how he'd lost Star and how angry he'd been at himself.

"I know how you felt," Howard said, thinking of his own exploits. "I guess we both have to learn to use a little common sense."

They eagerly asked and answered questions about each other. Joe wanted to know what it was like living in a big city since he'd never seen one. Howard was curious about the reservation and ranching. He listened intently when Joe spoke of his hopes for the High Elk herd.

"Look," Howard said as the High Elk house came into view, "aren't there two cars at your place?"

"Yes," agreed Joe, peering ahead. "Mom and Dad must be home early and—oh, hurry! It must be Mr. Iron Cloud and the man from the university."

Howard kicked the horse into a canter as Joe told him of the mysterious bundle and how he wanted to be present when it was opened.

Riding up fast into the yard they saw that the whole family, Mr. Iron Cloud, and a tall, gray-haired white man were gathered around the horse shed.

"Śungwiye!" yelled Joe. "Has she had a colt?"

"No, not yet," answered William, emerging from the mare's stall. "But I don't think it will be long. No," he said, taking Joe's arm as the boy started into the shed, "we'll leave her alone. She knows what to do and our presence will just make her nervous. Come into the house now. We'll check on her in a little while."

"Gosh, Dad, I can't begin to sit still. Oh, man, everything happens at once!"

Joe's father laughed at the boy's agitation, "I know, but don't you want to greet Mr. Iron Cloud and Dr. Scott who are here to open the High Elk bundle?"

"How do you do," said the tall white man. "I understand you've been having a lot of excitement around here."

"Hello, Joe. I'm glad you found your filly," greeted Mr. Iron Cloud.

Joe, remembering his manners, shook hands with the men. "Hello, Dr. Scott, Mr. Iron Cloud. I'm sure glad you're here. I guess this has been about the most exciting and worried time of my life!"

Laughing at Joe, the group moved into the house, but Joe noticed that Howard stayed behind.

"Dad, I told Howard about the High Elk thing," Joe said, wanting his new friend and relative to share the family's discovery.

William turned and called, "Come with us, Howard. This is your heritage too."

The High Elk Treasure

THE GROUP QUIETLY SEATED themselves around the kitchen table. Grandma brought the bundle, from which she had gently taken the buffalo hide, and placed it in the center of the table. She remained standing, a little distance from them. "*Tehinda*," she murmured.

"Now, *Ina*," William said soothingly, "the hundred years are almost over and I believe old High Elk only meant to keep his secret hidden until the danger of punishment was past."

"Open it, Joe," he said, motioning to his son. "You should have the honor, since you discovered it."

"No, I can't," Joe said, shaking his head. "I'm too nervous. Dr. Scott, you open it."

William nodded at the white man to go ahead. Dr. Scott began to undo the leather thongs, but they were rotten and fell apart in his hands.

"Was it in this condition when you found it?" he asked Joe.

"Yes. It was buried in the wall of the cave, and looked just like it does now."

Worriedly, Dr. Scott shook his head, "I hope its contents are in better condition than the outer covering. I imagine the cave is a damp place since it is so near the creek."

"No," William said. "The cave is well above the water line and dry."

The thongs off, Dr. Scott began to carefully unroll the rawhide. There were several layers of it; some peeled away easily, but in spots it tore away as if it had been glued together.

"It seems to have been partially sealed with something. It is a sticky, oily substance, I'm not sure, but it may be creosote."

"It might be the tar pitch of a pine tree," guessed William. "The old Indians knew how to use it for waterproofing."

"That could be," said Dr. Scott. "I'll have it chemically analyzed, but whatever it is, it seems to have protected the inner layer of the rawhide." He removed the last of the outer covering and disclosed a bulky, oblong, envelope-shaped bag. "Why it's a parfleche," he said, excitement sounding in his voice.

The parfleche was a heavy duty storage packet used to store dried food or personal belongings. They were made, as was this one, by folding a single wet sheet of rawhide into the desired form.

"Why, you can still see the design on it," marveled Marlene.

"Yes, someone, probably High Elk's wife, took great pains to paint it carefully as well as artistically," said Dr. Scott, gently lifting the parfleche to examine it. "It is in surprisingly good shape, just a little decay on the corners."

He opened it and found another leather-wrapped package inside.

"This," he said taking the smaller bundle out, "is of tanned hide, probably elk or deer. It is very soft and smells sweet," he mused as he unrolled it. The pungent odor reached the group gathered around the table. Dr. Scott found the source of the spicy scent in a braided stalk of grass rolled in the leather wrapping.

"Sweet grass," he said. "Didn't the Indians use this as we use a sachet?"

"Yes," answered Marlene, "we still do. We have some that Grandma braided in our storage trunk."

Dr. Scott nodded. "Now," he breathed, "we come to whatever was precious enough to merit such care."

A smaller piece of tanned hide was rolled within the outer one. Gently, with extreme care, he spread it flat on the table.

"Look, there are pictures painted on it," Joe said. "What is it?"

"This is fantastic!" The historian was amazed at the discovery. "It is a pictograph narrative." He bent closer to examine it. "It must be the record of some important event, but it is too small to be of the Winter Count type."

"Aren't those soldiers?" Joe asked, placing his finger on the crudely drawn figures which seemed to be scattered in one section. "They look like they have the kind of uniforms that the army used to wear long ago."

"You're right," Dr. Scott answered, clearly excited. "And look here, in the center must be the general. Good Heavens," he said unbelievingly, "I think this is Custer and the drawing must be an account of the Battle of the Little Big Horn."

"It must be Custer," said William. "See, he is dressed differently than the soldiers. Didn't he wear a buckskin jacket?"

"Where?" Joe asked. "I don't see, which one?"

"Here," Dr. Scott said, putting his finger on the figure, "this one with the long yellow hair." Then pointing to another figure, "And this must be the Indian who shot him. See, he is holding a gun."

There was a mournful wail from Grandma, who covered her face with her hands. She was still afraid.

"How can you tell who it is?" asked Joe. "His face is all covered with what looks like drops of water or blood."

"Rain-In-The-Face," said the historian softly.

He was silent, gazing at the wondering faces around him.

"I won't be sure until I review the information on this battle, but there was a Sioux warrior called Rain-In-The-Face who was suspected of killing both General Custer and his brother. In fact, if I remember right, I believe he bragged of doing so. But there were many conflicting stories from Indians who were at the Little Big Horn, and those who may have really known, would not say. . . ."

". . . for a hundred years," William finished for him.

"Yes, one hundred years," repeated Dr. Scott. "Did High Elk participate in this battle?" he asked William.

William looked at his mother who had uncovered her eyes. "So my husband was told," she said quietly.

"High Elk must have made this record of the killing of Custer," the historian said, "and then to keep the vow he and other warriors made, he buried it for safekeeping in the cave."

"Did you know of this, *Ina?*" William asked his mother.

She nodded. "My husband told me, whose father told him. I was to tell you before I died."

"This can't be true," Mr. Iron Cloud broke in. "My great-grandfather, who was in this battle, said that Custer killed himself."

"As I said," Mr. Scott looked at Mr. Iron Cloud, "there were so many conflicting stories of what happened on that day. There was also much confusion and a thick dust enveloped the battlefield, making observation difficult."

"What do you suppose this means?" asked Joe, who had been studying the pictures. "This man with antlers on his head, who looks like he's taking funny steps, he's leading a horse—why it looks like Śungwiye." He looked at his father. "Do you think that's supposed to be High Elk leading a horse away from the battlefield?"

"Why, I know about this," Howard said in surprise. "Grandpa told me that near the end of the battle High Elk found the wounded mare and led her to safety. Man, I never thought I would ever see a picture of it."

"Yes," agreed Grandma, "the mare was taken from the soldiers on that day. She was wounded in the leg and lamed after it healed."

"I thought he stole the horse from another tribe," Joe said.

At this, his grandmother shook her head, "No. That was the story he told to prevent punishment."

"Didn't the army put big 'U.S.' brands on their stock?" Howard asked Dr. Scott. "I wonder how High Elk kept the soldiers from seeing it."

"Yes," Dr. Scott answered, "the animals were branded. Do you know about this, Mrs. High Elk?" he asked Grandma.

She shook her head.

"But look," Mr. Iron Cloud interrupted. "How could High Elk know who killed Custer if he was leading a horse away from the battleground? See, he has his back to the whole thing."

The group around the table fell silent.

"Gee," Joe said quietly, "this is more mysterious than ever. What *does* it all mean?" he asked, looking at his father and then at Dr. Scott.

Dr. Scott smiled, "It means that you have found a very valuable historical record, even with all its mystery. It is probably worth hundreds, or perhaps thousands of dollars, depending on which museum wants it badly enough."

Wordlessly the family stared at him.

"The horses, the herd . . ." William murmured, thinking of what the money could do.

Dr. Scott began rolling the leather back up. "If it meets with your approval, I would like to take this, and the wrappings, back to the university with me. I need more time to examine it and do a thorough study. When I have done so I will make a public announcement of the discovery. Can I assume you would sell the pictograph?"

William looked at his wife, who smiled at him, then at the tribal chairman. "Frank," he began and then he said to Dr. Scott, "I don't know."

Mr. Iron Cloud cleared his throat, "The tribe wouldn't be able to pay you anything, Will, but we would be honored to have this in our new Tribal Museum."

"Well, think about it," said Dr. Scott. "There will be plenty of time in which to make a decision. In the meantime, I will give you a receipt showing that I am borrowing the pictograph from you. I hope you will trust me to take good care of it."

"Dad! Dad!" Marie came screaming into the house. Startled, William leapt to his feet. In his concentration on the unwrapping of the bundle, he hadn't noticed the little girl's absence.

"Dad," she called again. "Šungwiye had her baby. Oh, come see!"

The excited group quickly started to go outside. Marie took her mother's hand.

"Mama, I hid behind the shed and peeked, where Šungwiye wouldn't see me. Mama," Marie said, full of wonder, "I saw it born."

"Yahoo!" Joe yelled, following his father out the door. "Come on, Howard," he called to his cousin, "see a new High Elk horse!"

William ran into the shed and knelt by the mare to examine the new foal.

"It is a male," he announced.

Joe was close to tears as he watched Šungwiye gently licking and nuzzling the colt which lay snuggled close to her side. The mare carefully stood and began nudging the perfect little horse to his feet. He struggled to untangle his long, thin legs, not yet sure what they were for. He gained his footing on delicate front hooves, spraddled before him. Šungwiye nudged encouragingly at his rear, and awkwardly, but surely, he stood. He swayed and staggered, staring curiously at the people watching his progress. He took a cautious step, turned to his mother and began to nurse.

"Oh, isn't he beautiful," Marie said softly. "Why he looks just like Star."

The colt did resemble his sister. The same golden color, dark now with the wetness of his birth, the same star-shaped blaze on his forehead and four identical white stockings.

"What will we call him?" asked Marie. "He can't be 'Star' too."

"He should have a Lakota name," said Joe. "One that means 'hope' or 'beginning,' because that's what he is, isn't he Dad?"

William nodded, his throat too tight to speak.

"The colt will be called '*Otokahe*,'" said Grandma. "Beginning."

Related Readings

Dee Brown	from *The War for the Black Hills*	historical nonfiction	50
Monty Roberts	from *The Man Who Listens to Horses*	informative nonfiction	57
Leroy V. Quintana	The Legacy II	poem	68
Margaret Walker	Lineage	poem	69
as told by Lame Deer	A Legend of Devil's Tower	folktale	70
Jean Fritz	from *Homesick: My Own Story*	memoir	73

Dee Brown

from

The War for the Black Hills

To the Sioux, the Black Hills, or Paha Sapa, in what is now South Dakota, was sacred land. The United States government had signed treaties with the Sioux promising that the Black Hills would remain forever under Indian ownership. However, after gold was discovered there and white prospectors invaded the area, the government decided to claim the land. The Indians fought to protect their rights to the land, but eventually the government sent soldiers to protect the miners. Independent groups of Sioux were ordered to report to government agencies on local reservations by January 31, 1876. This passage from the book Bury My Heart at Wounded Knee *describes how the Sioux responded to the order and eventually did battle with the U.S. military forces near the Little Bighorn River.*

WHEN RUNNERS WENT out from the agencies late in December to warn the non-agency chiefs[1] to come in, heavy snows blanketed the northern Plains. Blizzards and severe cold made it impossible for some couriers[2] to return until weeks after the January 31 deadline;[3] it

---

1. **non-agency chiefs** leaders of Indians who were not living on reservations
2. **couriers** messengers; runners
3. **January 31 deadline** date when all Indians off reservations were to come in and report to U.S. government agents or face military action

would have been impossible to move women and children by ponies and travois.[4] Had a few thousand "hostiles"[5] somehow managed to reach the agencies, they would have starved there. On the reservations during the late winter, food supplies were so short that hundreds of Indians left in March to go north in search of game to supplement their meager government rations.

In January a courier found Sitting Bull camped near the mouth of the Powder. The Hunkpapa[6] chief sent the messenger back to the agent, informing him that he would consider the order to come in, but could not do so until the Moon When the Green Grass Is Up.

Crazy Horse's Oglalas were in winter camp near Bear Butte, where the Thieves' Road[7] came into the Black Hills from the north. During the spring it would be a good place to make up raiding parties to go against the miners violating *Paha Sapa*. When agency couriers made their way through the snow to Crazy Horse, he told them politely that he could not come until the cold went away. "It was very cold," a young Oglala remembered afterward, "and many of our people and ponies would have died in the snow. Also, we were in our own country and were doing no harm."

* * * * * *

As the weather warmed, the tribes began moving northward in search of wild game and fresh grass. Along the way they were joined by bands of Brulès, Sans Arcs, Blackfoot Sioux, and additional Cheyennes. Most of these Indians had left their reservations in accordance with their treaty rights as hunters, and those who had heard of the January 31 ultimatum[8] either considered it as only another idle[9] threat of the Great Father's agents or did not believe it applied to peaceful Indians. "Many young men were anxious to go for fighting

---

4. **travois** crude sleds consisting of two poles joined by a net or platform and pulled by horse or dog
5. **"hostiles"** Indians not on reservations
6. **Hunkpapa** a specific tribe of Sioux, as are the Oglalas and Minneconjou
7. **Thieves' Road** the trail, first cut by General Custer and his supply wagons, that white prospectors followed into the Black Hills
8. **ultimatum** deadline; last chance to avoid military action
9. **idle** worthless; insignificant

the soldiers," said the Cheyenne warrior Wooden Leg. "But the chiefs and old men all urged us to keep away from the white men."

* * * * * *

They did not know until the morning of June 24 that Long Hair Custer was prowling along the Rosebud. Next morning scouts reported that the soldiers had crossed the last high ridge between the Rosebud and the Indian camp and were marching toward the Little Bighorn.

The news of Custer's approach came to the Indians in various ways:

"I and four women were a short distance from the camp digging wild turnips," said Red Horse, one of the Sioux council chiefs. "Suddenly one of the women attracted my attention to a cloud of dust rising a short distance from camp. I soon saw that the soldiers were charging the camp. To the camp I and the women ran. When I arrived a person told me to hurry to the council lodge. The soldiers charged so quickly that we could not talk. We came out of the council lodge and talked in all directions. The Sioux mount horses, take guns, and go fight the soldiers. Women and children mount horses and go, meaning to get out of the way."

Pte-San-Waste-Win, a cousin of Sitting Bull, was one of the young women digging turnips that morning. She said the soldiers were six to eight miles distant when first sighted. "We could see the flashing of their sabers and saw that there were very many soldiers in the party." The soldiers first seen by Pte-San-Waste-Win and other Indians in the middle of the camp were those in Custer's battalion. These Indians were not aware of Major Marcus Reno's surprise attack against the south end of camp until they heard rifle fire from the direction of the Blackfoot Sioux lodges. "Like that the soldiers were upon us. Through the tepee poles their bullets rattled. . . . The women and children cried, fearing they would be killed, but the men, the Hunkpapa and Blackfeet, the Oglala and Minneconjou, mounted their horses and raced to the Blackfoot tepees. We could still see the soldiers of Long Hair marching along in the distance, and our men, taken by surprise, and from a point whence[10] they had not expected to

---

10. **whence** from which

be attacked, went singing the song of battle into the fight behind the Blackfoot village.

* * * * * *

The war chief who rallied the Indians and turned back Reno's attack was a muscular, full-chested, thirty-six-year-old Hunkpapa named Pizi, or Gall. Gall had grown up in the tribe as an orphan. While still a young man he distinguished himself as a hunter and warrior, and Sitting Bull adopted him as a younger brother. Some years before, while the commissioners were attempting to persuade the Sioux to take up farming as a part of the treaty of 1868, Gall went to Fort Rice to speak for the Hunkpapas. "We were born naked," he said, "and have been taught to hunt and live on the game. You tell us that we must learn to farm, live in one house, and take on your ways. Suppose the people living beyond the great sea should come and tell you that you must stop farming and kill your cattle, and take your houses and lands, what would you do? Would you not fight them?" In the decade following that speech, nothing changed Gall's opinion of the white man's self-righteous arrogance, and by the summer of 1876 he was generally accepted by the Hunkpapas as Sitting Bull's lieutenant, the war chief of the tribe.

Reno's first onrush caught several women and children in the open, and the cavalry's flying bullets virtually wiped out Gall's family. "It made my heart bad," he told a newspaperman some years later. "After that I killed all my enemies with the hatchet." His description of the tactics used to block Reno was equally terse:[11] "Sitting Bull and I were at the point where Reno attacked. Sitting Bull was big medicine. The women and children were hastily moved downstream. . . . The women and children caught the horses for the bucks to mount them; the bucks mounted and charged back Reno and checked him, and drove him into the timber."

In military terms, Gall turned Reno's flank and forced him into the woods. He then frightened Reno into making a hasty retreat which the Indians quickly turned into a rout. The result made it possible for Gall to divert hundreds of warriors for a frontal attack against

---

11. **terse** brief; concise

Custer's column, while Crazy Horse and Two Moon struck the flank and rear.

Meanwhile Pte-San-Waste-Win and the other women had been anxiously watching the Long Hair's soldiers across the river. "I could hear the music of the bugle and could see the column of soldiers turn to the left to march down to the river where the attack was to be made. . . . Soon I saw a number of Cheyennes ride into the river, then some young men of my band, then others, until there were hundreds of warriors in the river and running up into the ravine.[12] When some hundreds had passed the river and gone into the ravine, the others who were left, still a very great number, moved back from the river and waited for the attack. And I knew that the fighting men of the Sioux, many hundreds in number, were hidden in the ravine behind the hill upon which Long Hair was marching, and he would be attacked from both sides."

Kill Eagle, a Blackfoot Sioux chief, later said that the movement of Indians toward Custer's column was "like a hurricane . . . like bees swarming out of a hive." Hump, the Minneconjou comrade of Gall and Crazy Horse during the old Powder River days, said the first massive charge by the Indians caused the long-haired chief and his men to become confused. "The first dash the Indians made my horse was shot from under me and I was wounded—shot above the knee, and the ball came out at the hip, and I fell and lay right there." Crow King, who was with the Hunkpapas, said: "The greater portion of our warriors came together in their front and we rushed our horses on them. At the same time warriors rode out on each side of them and circled around them until they were surrounded." Thirteen-year-old Black Elk, watching from across the river, could see a big dust whirling on the hill, and then horses began coming out of it with empty saddles.

"The smoke of the shooting and the dust of the horses shut out the hill," Pte-San-Waste-Win said, "and the soldiers fired many shots, but the Sioux shot straight and the soldiers fell dead. The women crossed the river after the men of our village, and when we came to the hill there were no soldiers living and Long Hair lay dead among the rest. . . . The blood of the people was hot and their hearts bad, and they took no prisoners that day."

---

12. **ravine** long, deep hollow in the earth's surface; deep gully

Crow King said that all the soldiers dismounted when the Indians surrounded them. "They tried to hold on to their horses, but as we pressed closer they let go their horses. We crowded them toward our main camp and killed them all. They kept in order and fought like brave warriors as long as they had a man left."

According to Red Horse, toward the end of the fighting with Custer, "these soldiers became foolish, many throwing away their guns and raising their hands, saying, 'Sioux, pity us; take us prisoners.' The Sioux did not take a single soldier prisoner, but killed all of them; none were alive for even a few minutes."

Long after the battle, White Bull of the Minneconjous drew four pictographs showing himself grappling with and killing a soldier identified as Custer. Among others who claimed to have killed Custer were Rain-in-the-Face, Flat Hip, and Brave Bear. Red Horse said that an unidentified Santee warrior killed Custer. Most Indians who told of the battle said they never saw Custer and did not know who killed him. "We did not know till the fight was over that he was the white chief," Low Dog said.

In an interview given in Canada a year after the battle, Sitting Bull said that he never saw Custer, but that other Indians had seen and recognized him just before he was killed. "He did not wear his long hair as he used to wear it," Sitting Bull said. "It was short, but it was the color of the grass when the frost comes. . . . Where the last stand was made, the Long Hair stood like a sheaf of corn with all the ears fallen around him." But Sitting Bull did not say who killed Custer.

An Arapaho warrior who was riding with the Cheyennes said that Custer was killed by several Indians. "He was dressed in buckskin, coat and pants, and was on his hands and knees. He had been shot through the side, and there was blood coming from his mouth. He seemed to be watching the Indians moving around him. Four soldiers were sitting up around him, but they were all badly wounded. All the other soldiers were down. Then the Indians closed in around him, and I did not see any more."

Regardless of who had killed him, the Long Hair who made the Thieves' Road into the Black Hills was dead with all his men. Reno's soldiers, however, reinforced by those of Major Frederick Benteen, were dug in on a hill farther down the river. The Indians surrounded the hill completely and watched the soldiers through the night, and next morning started fighting them again. During the day, scouts sent out by the chiefs came back with warnings of many more soldiers marching in the direction of the Little Bighorn.

After a council it was decided to break camp. The warriors had expended most of their ammunition, and they knew it would be foolish to try to fight so many soldiers with bows and arrows. The women were told to begin packing, and before sunset they started up the valley toward the Bighorn Mountains, the tribes separating along the way and taking different directions.

from

The Man Who Listens to Horses

Monty Roberts

Monty Roberts, who is known as the Horse Whisperer, has a special talent for communicating with and training horses, a talent that he has continued to develop throughout his life.

THE FOLLOWING SUMMER was perhaps the finest of my life. I would spend much of it alone in the high desert, in what I came to see as an outdoor university. I was a freshman at Mustang U. But first I had to make some new arrangements with Doc Leach.

"What can I do for you, son?"

"I have an idea how to improve the wild horse race this year."

"You didn't do so badly for us last time."

"How about we reduce the number of mustangs we haul back here?"

"And that's to improve the race, is it?"

"Well," I explained, "I noticed that you didn't use all hundred-and-fifty head. You picked out the best two-thirds of them."

"That's right, we did."

"What if we choose the best two-thirds of them up there in Nevada instead of down here in Salinas? Then we'd only be transporting a hundred head instead of one-fifty, and we could lower the overhead."

Even at fourteen, I had a pretty firm grasp of cost.

Doc Leach looked down at me. "Who's going to judge the best one hundred head—you?"

"That's right, sir. Then we can avoid bringing the lactating[1] mares and the older animals in the first place."

Doc Leach smiled. "You've got a point, I have to admit."

I recommended that we gather 500 head and select the best 100 adolescent colts and fillies. ("Adolescent" in mustang terms means an animal three to five years old, since the limited nutrition and harsh desert environment delay their maturity. Mustangs cover vast territories to feed, and the saying is that they can graze—at twenty miles an hour.)

I paid a trucker to transport myself, Brownie, Sergeant, and Oriel up to the Campbell Ranch. Ralph and Vivian Carter agreed to join me later on this adventure; the helpers and truck convoy would come up with them. But for three weeks I would be alone in the Nevada desert with the mustangs. I would have the time to move slowly and observe them without interfering in any way. The Campbell Ranch had prior information on the location of family groups, which were sometimes ten miles apart. I intended to bring each family group toward the trap in the barranca[2] one by one, very slowly, observing them as I went.

Once again, I was glad to have Brownie as one of my saddle horses for this all-important experience. I patted his neck as we rode out over the high desert ground. Oriel and Sergeant walked along behind, and in addition I had our black-and-white stock dog, called Bobby, three pairs of binoculars (two spares, for I would have been lost without them), a handgun and a rifle.

When we reached the first horizon I twisted around in my saddle and watched the outbuildings of the Campbell Ranch disappear from sight as we moved down the opposite side of the slope. We were on our own.

It felt good to be riding across this open ground again, with its rocky barrancas where the cottonwood and aspen trees grew. I would have to be extra vigilant for rattlesnakes. Worse were the invisible crevices: you might be galloping across what looked like a flat, unbroken expanse of desert in pursuit of a herd when, suddenly, a six-foot crevice yawned at your horse's feet. The mustangs, who usually spotted you before you spotted them, used these depressions cleverly.

---

1. **lactating** milk-producing
2. **barranca** deep ravine; steep cliff

They would travel in them at the slightest suspicion of danger, and from my vantage a mile away it seemed that the horses in my sights had suddenly vanished.

My father was right, at least, about the weather: the days were hot, the nights cold. Occasionally, rainstorms would lash me and the horses for an hour. Big, billowy, high-desert clouds would give rise to electrical storms. I was living on a diet mostly of jerky—a cured meat—plus pancake mix and salami, as well as oranges.

To find the first family group of horses, I had to consider their food source. The mustangs would eat the sage and the chamise if they were desperate, but they preferred the gramma, brome, and rye grasses.

When I caught up with my first group, my aim was to integrate with the herd as closely as I could. Either they would accept me as no threat, which meant staying more than a mile distant, or I could try to get closer without their knowing I was there. The latter option quickly evaporated. The horses caught my scent from a mile away and began to move off. They were little more than dots on the plateau, and already they were going away.

I left Oriel, my bay packhorse, behind because he was proving rather clumsy and often stumbled over stones, the noise of which carried over vast distances—not that he cared. I was beginning to wonder about this Oriel character. His ears were always at half-mast, neither forward nor backward. He was either a deep thinker or a little dumb, maybe both.

After lightly hobbling[3] him and leaving Sergeant to keep him company, I continued on foot, leading Brownie. We used the barrancas as cover and stayed downwind, moving quietly. Given the time to move slowly and think about what was happening, I was surprised by how hypersensitive the herd was to our presence. If Brownie just scuffed a rock, I could see their ears flick in our direction.

I could get within a quarter mile of the herd, but no closer. I was running out of cover and even though I was downwind of them, they would cede[4] us no more ground. Brownie and I settled down by a cottonwood tree and I counted the horses, trying to log their markings so I could distinguish one from another.

My binoculars were key. When I see young people today strapping

---

3. **hobbling** tying two feet together to hamper movement
4. **cede** give; surrender

on virtual reality helmets, entranced by the world they enter, I am reminded of how I felt when I looked through binoculars at that herd of wild horses. They seemed close enough to touch. I could see subtle shifts of the eyes, ears, tongue. These were pure movements, untainted by human intervention. That day I would watch for eight continuous hours.

I noticed, in particular, the dun[5] mare. Older than most of the others, with a heavier belly that hinted at many pregnancies, she seemed to issue a lot of commands. She ordered her group to move off. She started, the others followed. She stopped, they did likewise. It seemed she was the wisest, and they knew it.

What I was observing, in fact, was the dominant mare. Many people likely still think that the stallion runs the show. The breeding or dominant stallion, sometimes called the alpha male or lead male, will skirt the herd and defend it from marauders.[6] His motivation is to prevent anyone or anything from stealing his harem. But it was the dun mare who was in charge of the day-to-day running of this group. There was no mistaking it.

And then I saw an extraordinary sequence of events. A light bay colt was behaving badly. He was about twenty months old, I guessed, with a vast amount of feathering around his fetlocks and down the backs of his legs, and a mane running down well below his neckline. He took a run at a filly and gave her a kick. The filly cowered and hobbled off, and the colt looked pleased with himself. . . .

Then he committed another crime. A little foal approached him, moving his mouth in a suckling action to indicate he was no threat but subservient. Just a foal. That cut no ice with this colt; he launched himself at his younger cousin and took a bite out of the foal's backside. The bay colt was a terrorist. Immediately after the attack, he pretended nothing had happened; he went neutral, as though trying to avoid blame.

Each time he behaved badly, the dun mare—the matriarch[7]—weaved a little closer to him. I became certain that she was watching for any more of this behavior. She showed no apparent sign of

---

5. **dun** dull grayish-brown

6. **marauders** thieves

7. **matriarch** female who rules her family or tribe

interest, but she had left her station and was edging closer to him all the time.

The mare witnessed about four such episodes before she finally made her move. Now she stood within twenty yards. Still, the cream-colored colt could not help himself: he launched at a grown mare, grabbed the nape of her neck, and bit down hard.

The dun mare did not hesitate. In an instant she went from neutral to full-blown anger; she pinned her ears back and ran at him, knocking him down. As he struggled to his feet, she whirled and knocked him down again. While this chastisement[8] unfolded, the other members apparently took no notice.

The dun mare ended by driving the colt 300 yards from the herd and left him there, alone. Amazed, I tried to fathom[9] what I was seeing. The mare took up a position on the edge of the herd to keep him in exile. She kept her eyes on his and faced up to him. She was freezing him out.

It terrified the colt to be left alone. For a flight animal, this was tantamount to[10] a death sentence; the predators will get any horse long separated from the group. He walked back and forth, his head close to the ground, several times executing this strange, uncomfortable gait. It looked like a sign of obedience, similar to a human's bow.

Then the colt made his way around to the other side of the herd and attempted to sneak back in that way, but the dun mare had followed his circle. Again she drove him out, running at him until he had fled another 300 yards. Returning to her post on the edge of the herd, she kept her body square on his, and never once took her eye off him.

He stood there, and I noticed a lot of licking and chewing going on, although with all this drama he had eaten nothing. I remembered the foal and how he had snapped his mouth in an obvious signal of humility, as though he were saying, "I'm not a threat to you." Was this colt now saying the same thing to his matriarch?

By this time, it was getting dark, and I would have to get back to the other horses. I wanted the moon bright that night; I wanted desperately to see how the tale would end. I scooped up Brownie's reins and rode back to where Sergeant and Oriel were waiting. My

---

8. **chastisement** punishment
9. **fathom** understand thoroughly
10. **tantamount to** equal to; equivalent to

intention was to camp there and continue observing the dialogue between mare and colt.

When I got back, Oriel was standing with his nose in a bush. Then he lifted his head sharply, his whole body tense with surprise. A cloud of bees surrounded his head. This was an emergency, for the horse was clearly being stung. Oriel took a few paces backward and then tried a couple more sideways. He tried it with his head held low and then jerked it up again.

No luck.

Then he shook himself like a dog emerging from water. The bees still hovered, a cloud hooked on a mountaintop. This was a puzzle, and Oriel had nearly run out of tricks. There was only one left: he tossed his head up and down, evidently figuring that if he did this long enough the bees would get bored and leave, which is what they did.

Oriel did not seem unduly perturbed[11] by the experience. It was one of life's many mysteries: the one and only time I ever saw a bee swarm take such a shine to a horse's head. . . .

The sun now sank surprisingly fast down the western slope of the sky, as though itself desiring rest from a hard day's work. I made camp and hurried to settle Brownie, Sergeant, and Oriel with their feed.

From its place in that vast sky, the moon cast the landscape in a new and surprisingly generous light. I picked up my binoculars and found I could see clearly for quite a distance. I did not realize it then, but my night vision was likely helped by the fact that I am totally color-blind. I know that the color of the high desert is dove-gray only because others have told me. Mine is a rare condition, quite separate from the more common one in which an individual cannot properly distinguish colors.

When I was young, no one believed that I could see only in black and white, but I have subsequently learned that I see in a way very different from normally sighted people.

Oliver Sacks, in his study of "The Case of the Colorblind Painter," describes how his subject had a car accident that caused him to lose all perception of color. But along with that terrible loss came an unexpected gift: "People's figures might be visible and recognizable half a mile off . . . his vision had become much sharper, 'that of an

---

11. **perturbed** upset; alarmed

eagle.'" Distressed by his condition, the artist became nocturnal and at night his extraordinary vision allowed him to identify a license plate four blocks away.

Using the binoculars, I caught sight of my herd. To my astonishment, the dun mare was now grooming the troublesome colt. She was giving him little scrapes on his neck and hindquarters with her teeth, and generally fussing over him. She had let him back in; now she was keeping him close by and giving him a lot of attention. She worked away at the root of his tail, hips, and withers.[12]

Purgatory[13] was behind him. This was heaven.

As it turned out, night was a better time to watch the wild herds. Mustangs fear attacks from predators mostly at dawn and dusk; at night they relax and their social interaction is more marked. It became a habit to watch them by the light of the moon, and I would usually sleep from about one-thirty A.M. until five-thirty A.M.

For the next two summers, I would round up mustangs for the Salinas rodeo, and nothing I saw ever matched the exchange between the dun mare and that light bay colt. It was educational to watch the matriarch disciplining young, adolescent horses because so much happened. The youthful energy and inexperience of the gang of adolescents drove them to make mistakes, much like the young of any species.

Often, like a child, the colt would reoffend immediately after being let back in, to test the disciplinary system and to gain back lost ground. He might fight another colt or bother the fillies. The dun mare came right back and disciplined him again. Each time he sinned she drove him out and kept him out before letting him back in and welcoming him into the group with extensive grooming. The third time he sinned, he practically owned up and exited by himself, grumbling about it but accepting his fate.

Then, finally, his teenage rebellion ceased. Now cloyingly[14] sweet, he had become a positive nuisance, wandering about and asking every horse, "Do you need any grooming?" when all they wanted was to be left alone to eat. For four days the dun mare had made the education of this awful brat her number-one priority, and it had paid off.

---

12. **withers** area on the back between the shoulder blades
13. **purgatory** place of temporary punishment
14. **cloyingly** displeasingly

As I watched the mare's training procedures with this adolescent and others, I began to understand the language she used, and it was exciting to recognize the exact sequence of signals that would pass between her and the younger horses. It really was a language—predictable, discernible,[15] and effective.

The silent aspect of her commands is worth dwelling on because we often underrate a language that uses a different medium from our own. As I was to learn much later, the most common form of communication on this planet takes place silently—in the dark of the deep sea, where animals use intricate lighting systems called bioluminescence to attract mates, ward off predators, attract prey, and otherwise convey all the signals necessary for their existence.

Body language is not confined to humans or horses; it constitutes the most common form of communication between all animate objects.

In the desert, the dun mare constantly schooled the foals and yearlings, and they responded to her, without a sound. The stallion's security system required near absolute silence, and his investigations of mating potential were also conducted soundlessly. The mustangs were happy with one another, upset with one another, guided and advised one another—all in silence.

I learned that in the equine universe, every degree of a horse's movement has a reason. Nothing is trivial, nothing is to be dismissed. A horse raised alone, I now know, will still speak Equus:[16] genetics imparts much of the language. But the lone horse's communication is dull, less defined. A mustang raised in the wild in a herd, on the other hand, displays as pure a form of the equine tongue as I could have hoped to find anywhere.

I would learn, much later, while starting horses in a round pen, a rich code of signs and subsigns. Keeping my mouth closed invited the horse's discomfort, opening it slightly was fine. Opening a fist on the side of my body away from the horse drew him in, while opening a fist close to him sent him away. Fingers open stirred one response, fingers closed another. Hands above my head with fingers splayed[17] provoked

---

15. **discernable** recognizable

16. **Equus** genus for any hoofed, herbivorous mammal, commonly used for horse by including donkey and zebra; here, the language used by horses

17. **splayed** spread

true panic (perhaps it triggers primordial[18] memories of cat claws). Whether I am moving, standing still, facing the horse, or away: all this matters as the horse reads my body language and I read his. I can now enumerate about one hundred or more signs the horse will respond to, and the vocabulary is still growing.

The key ingredient in the equine language is the positioning of the body and its direction of travel. The attitude of the body relative to the long axis of the spine and the short axis: this is critical to their vocabulary. It *is* their vocabulary.

When the dun mare squared up and faced the colt, she was holding up a Keep Out sign. If she showed him part of her long axis, he could begin to consider returning to the herd. But before she would say, "I forgive you," he had to say, "I'm sorry." If the colt paced with his nose close to the ground, then he was asking for a chance to end his isolation and to renegotiate his position with her. He was saying, "I am obedient, and I'm willing to listen." If he showed her the long axis of his body, then he was offering vulnerable areas to her and asking to be forgiven.

Their eye contact also spoke volumes. When she was holding him out there, she always kept one eye directly on his, sometimes for uncomfortably long periods of time. When her eye slid a short distance off his, he knew he might be allowed back in. I came to realize how subtle was this reading of eye contact. Even when I was unfamiliar to this herd, I could cause a horse to alter his direction and pace of movement by changing which part of his body I looked at—even from a distance.

When the colt trotted out to suffer his exile, he would throw his nose out in a circular motion. Translation: "I didn't intend to do that. I'm sorry. It wasn't my idea. It just happened. It was the other guy's fault." The dun mare had to judge whether or not to believe him. I could see her thinking about it. Sometimes she bought it, sometimes not. The licking and chewing action of the colt's mouth was a signal of penitence. He was saying to her, "Look, I'm a herbivore. I'm no threat to you. I'm eating over here."

Observing all this, I could make sense of the "yo-yo effect" once described by my Uncle Ray. Cherokee hunters had for centuries exploited the tendency of prey animals, once chased, to circle back and

---

18. **primordial** primitive; from earliest time

"hunt" the hunter. Press the young horse away, and his instinct is to return. The dun mare advanced on him, then retreated. When I made this connection between the mare's discipline and Uncle Ray's story, it was as if synapses[19] in my brain all fired simultaneously. A term sprang to my mind—"Advance and Retreat."

In time, I would grasp just how exact a language it was. There were precise messages, whole phrases and sentences that always meant the same thing, always had the same effect.

Perhaps, it occurred to me, I could use the same silent system of communication myself. If I understood how to do it, I could effectively cross over the boundary between human (the ultimate fight animal) and horse (the flight animal). Using their language, their system of communication, I could create a strong bond of trust. I would achieve cross-species communication.

"Advance and Retreat" also offered a psychological explanation for why horses are "into pressure" animals. In my twenties, during a short career riding bucking horses, I once waited in the chute on a horse who was leaning hard on one side, pinching my leg against the boards. Six cowboys were pushing against the horse's body trying to move him over, but the harder they pushed, the more the horse leaned. Finally, one wise old horseman chanced by and put one finger against the horse's *other* side, as if pushing against it. Instantly, the horse moved into that little bit of pressure and my pinched leg was just as instantly grateful.

Horses, as a natural response, do not move away from pressure, they move into it—particularly if the pressure is applied to their flanks. The wild dogs that prey on horses on every continent attack the horse's belly, aiming to tear a hole in the stomach wall so the intestines will drop out. The dogs can then fall back and track the horse, confident that a meal is imminent.

Once flight is no longer a clear option, the horse's best defense is not to run but to turn into the onslaught and kick: if they run from a bite, their skin will more likely tear. I am convinced that this explains a phenomenon recognized by all good trainers: poke a forefinger into a horse's side and he will move against the pressure rather than away from it. It is perhaps the single most important thing to remember in training horses. *Horses are into pressure animals.*

---

19. **synapses** spaces between nerve cells through which nerve impulses are transmitted

Go into pain, nature told the horse. And the horse heeded the message. Over the years I would expand my Equus vocabulary, but even the more refined signs would exist within this all-important umbrella concept of Advance and Retreat that I learned at the age of thirteen.

**Leroy V.
Quintana**

The Legacy II

*Learning about past generations can help us more
fully understand who we are.*

Grandfather never went to school
spoke only a few words of English,
a quiet man; when he talked
talked about simple things

5   planting corn or about the weather
sometimes about herding sheep as a child.
One day pointed to the four directions
taught me their names
    El Norte
10 Poniente   Oriente
    El Sud

He spoke their names as if they were
one of only a handful of things
a man needed to know

15 Now I look back
only two generations removed
realize I am nothing but a poor fool
who went to college

trying to find my way back
20 to the center of the world
where grandfather stood
that day.

Margaret Walker | # Lineage

My grandmothers were strong,
They followed plows and bent to toil.
They moved through fields sowing seed.
They touched earth and grain grew.
5   They were full of sturdiness and singing.

My grandmothers are full of memories—
Smelling of soap and onions and wet clay
With veins rolling roughly over quick hands
They have many clean words to say.
10   My grandmothers were strong.
Why am I not as they?

As told by Lame Deer

A Legend of Devil's Tower

Many cultures have myths or legends, passed down from generation to generation, that help preserve their history and heritage. This legend explains how a famous Wyoming landmark came to be.

OUT OF THE PLAINS OF WYOMING rises Devil's Tower. It is really a rock, visible for a hundred miles around, an immense cone of basalt[1] which seems to touch the clouds. It sticks out of the flat prairie as if someone had pushed it up from underground.

Of course, Devil's Tower is a white man's name. We have no devil in our beliefs and got along well all these many centuries without him. You people invented the devil and, as far as I am concerned, you can keep him. But everybody these days knows that towering rock by this name, so Devil's Tower it is. No use telling you its Indian name. Most tribes call it Bear Rock. There is a reason for that—if you see it, you will notice on its sheer sides many, many streaks and gashes running straight up and down, like scratches made by giant claws.

Well, long, long ago, two young Indian boys found themselves lost in the prairie. You know how it is. They had played shinny ball[2] and whacked it a few hundred yards out of the village. And then they had shot their toy bows still farther out into the sagebrush. And then they had heard a small animal make a noise and had gone to investigate. They had come to a stream with many colorful pebbles and followed

---

1. **basalt** dark volcanic rock
2. **shinny ball** simple form of hockey, especially as played by children

that for a while. They had come to a hill and wanted to see what was on the other side. On the other side they saw a herd of antelope and, of course, had to track them for a while. When they got hungry and thought it was time to go home, the two boys found that they didn't know where they were. They started off in the direction where they thought their village was, but only got farther and farther away from it. At last they curled up beneath a tree and went to sleep.

They got up the next morning and walked some more, still headed the wrong way. They ate some wild berries and dug up wild turnips, found some chokecherries, and drank water from streams. For three days they walked toward the west. They were footsore, but they survived. Oh, how they wished that their parents, or aunts and uncles, or elder brothers and sisters would find them. But nobody did.

On the fourth day the boys suddenly had a feeling that they were being followed. They looked around and in the distance saw Mato, the bear. This was no ordinary bear, but a giant grizzly so huge that the two boys would make only a small mouthful for him, but he had smelled the boys and wanted that mouthful. He kept coming close, and the earth trembled as he gathered speed.

The boys started running, looking for a place to hide, but there was no such place and the grizzly was much, much faster than they. They stumbled, and the bear was almost upon them. They could see his red, wide-open jaws full of enormous, wicked teeth. They could smell his hot, evil breath.

The boys were old enough to have learned to pray, and they called upon Wakan Tanka, the Creator: "Tunkashila, Grandfather, have pity, save us."

All at once the earth shook and began to rise. The boys rose with it. Out of the earth came a cone of rock going up, up, up until it was more than a thousand feet high. And the boys were on top of it.

Mato the bear was disappointed to see his meal disappearing into the clouds. Have I said he was a giant bear? This grizzly was so huge that he could almost reach to the top of the rock when he stood on his hind legs. Almost, but not quite. His claws were as large as a tipi's lodge poles. Frantically Mato dug his claws into the side of the rock, trying to get up, trying to get those boys. As he did so, he made big scratches in the sides of the towering rock. But the stone was too slippery; Mato could not get up. He tried every spot, every side. He scratched up the rock all around, but it was no use. The boys watched him wearing himself out, getting tired, giving up. They finally saw him going away, a huge, growling, grunting mountain of fur disappearing over the horizon.

The boys were saved. Or were they? How were they to get down? They were humans, not birds who could fly. Some ten years ago, mountain climbers tried to conquer Devil's Tower. They had ropes, and iron hooks called pitons to nail themselves to the rock face, and they managed to get up. But they couldn't get down. They were marooned on that giant basalt cone, and they had to be taken off in a helicopter.

In the long-ago days the Indians had no helicopters. So how did the two boys get down? The legend does not tell us, but we can be sure that the Great Spirit didn't save those boys only to let them perish of hunger and thirst on the top of the rock.

Well, Wanblee, the eagle, has always been a friend to our people. So it must have been the eagle that let the boys grab hold of him and carried them safely back to their village. Or do you know another way?

from
Homesick:My Own Story

Jean Fritz

Jean Fritz, who grew up in China, is keenly aware of how important her American heritage is to her.

IN MY FATHER'S STUDY there was a large globe with all the countries of the world running around it. I could put my finger on the exact spot where I was and had been ever since I'd been born. And I was on the wrong side of the globe. I was in China in a city named Hankow, a dot on a crooked line that seemed to break the country right in two. The line was really the Yangtse River, but who would know by looking at a map what the Yangtse River really was?

Orange-brown, muddy mustard-colored. And wide, wide, wide. With a river smell that was old and came all the way up from the bottom. Sometimes old women knelt on the riverbank, begging the River God to return a son or grandson who may have drowned. They would wail and beat the earth to make the River God pay attention, but I knew how busy the River God must be. All those people on the Yangtse River! Coolies[1] hauling water. Women washing clothes. Houseboats swarming with old people and young, chickens and pigs. Big crooked-sailed junks[2] with eyes painted on their prows[3] so they could see where they were going. I loved the Yangtse River, but, of course, I belonged on the other side of the world. In America with my grandmother.

---

1. **coolies** unskilled Chinese laborers
2. **junks** Chinese (or Japanese) flat-bottomed boats with high sterns and lugsails or lateen sails
3. **prows** forward parts of ships

Twenty-five fluffy little yellow chicks hatched from our eggs today, my grandmother wrote.

I wrote my grandmother that I had watched a Chinese magician swallow three yards of fire.

The trouble with living on the wrong side of the world was that I didn't feel like a *real* American.

For instance. I could never be president of the United States. I didn't want to be president; I wanted to be a writer. Still, why should there be a *law* saying that only a person born in the United States could be president? It was as if I wouldn't be American enough.

Actually, I was American every minute of the day, especially during school hours. I went to a British school and every morning we sang "God Save the King." Of course the British children loved singing about their gracious king. Ian Forbes stuck out his chest and sang as if he were saving the king all by himself. Everyone sang. Even Gina Boss who was Italian. And Vera Sebastian who was so Russian she dressed the way Russian girls did long ago before the Revolution[4] when her family had to run away to keep from being killed.

But I wasn't Vera Sebastian. I asked my mother to write an excuse so I wouldn't have to sing, but she wouldn't do it. "When in Rome," she said, "do as the Romans do." What she meant was, "Don't make trouble. Just sing." So for a long time I did. I sang with my fingers crossed but still I felt like a traitor.

Then one day I thought: If my mother and father were really and truly in Rome, they wouldn't do what the Romans did at all. They'd probably try to get the Romans to do what *they* did, just as they were trying to teach the Chinese to do what Americans did. (My mother even gave classes in American manners.)

So that day I quit singing. I kept my mouth locked tight against the king of England. Our teacher, Miss Williams, didn't notice at first. She stood in front of the room, using a ruler for a baton, striking each syllable so hard it was as if she were making up for the times she had nothing to strike.

(Miss Williams was pinch-faced and bossy. Sometimes I wondered what had ever made her come to China. "Maybe to try and catch a husband," my mother said.

A husband! Miss Williams!)

---

4. **the Revolution** the Russian Revolution of 1917

"Make him vic-tor-i-ous," the class sang. It was on the strike of "vic" that Miss Williams noticed. Her eyes lighted on my mouth and when we sat down, she pointed her ruler at me.

"Is there something wrong with your voice today, Jean?" she asked.

"No, Miss Williams."

"You weren't singing."

"No, Miss Williams. It is not my national anthem."

"It is the national anthem we sing here," she snapped. "You have always sung. Even Vera sings it."

I looked at Vera with the big blue bow tied on the top of her head. Usually I felt sorry for her but not today. At recess I might even untie that bow, I thought. Just give it a yank. But if I'd been smart, I wouldn't have been looking at Vera. I would have been looking at Ian Forbes and I would have known that, no matter what Miss Williams said, I wasn't through with the king of England.

Recess at the British School was nothing I looked forward to. Every day we played a game called prisoner's base, which was all running and shouting and shoving and catching. I hated the game, yet everyone played except Vera Sebastian. She sat on the sidelines under her blue bow like someone who had been dropped out of a history book. By recess I had forgotten my plans for that bow. While everyone was getting ready for the game, I was as usual trying to look as if I didn't care if I was the last one picked for a team or not. I was leaning against the high stone wall that ran around the schoolyard. I was looking up at a little white cloud skittering across the sky when all at once someone tramped down hard on my right foot. Ian Forbes. Snarling bulldog face. Heel grinding down on my toes. Head thrust forward the way an animal might before it strikes.

"You wouldn't sing it. So say it," he ordered. "Let me hear you say it."

I tried to pull my foot away but he only ground down harder.

"Say what?" I was telling my face please not to show what my foot felt.

"*God save the king.* Say it. Those four words. I want to hear you say it."

Although Ian Forbes was short, he was solid and tough and built for fighting. What was more, he always won. You had only to look at his bare knees between the top of his socks and his short pants to know that he would win. His knees were square. Bony and unbeatable. So of course it was crazy for me to argue with him.

"Why should I?" I asked. "Americans haven't said that since George the Third."[5]

He grabbed my right arm and twisted it behind my back.

"Say it," he hissed.

I felt the tears come to my eyes and I hated myself for the tears. I hated myself for not staying in Rome the way my mother had told me.

"I'll never say it," I whispered.

They were choosing sides now in the schoolyard and Ian's name was being called—among the first as always.

He gave my arm another twist. "You'll sing tomorrow," he snarled, "or you'll be bloody sorry."

As he ran off, I slid to the ground, my head between my knees.

Oh, Grandma, I thought, why can't I be there with you? I'd feed the chickens for you. I'd pump water from the well, the way my father used to do.

It would be almost two years before we'd go to America. I was ten years old now; I'd be twelve then. But how could I think about *years?* I didn't even dare to think about the next day. After school I ran all the way home, fast so I couldn't think at all.

Our house stood behind a high stone wall which had chips of broken glass sticking up from the top to keep thieves away. I flung open the iron gate and threw myself through the front door.

"I'm home!" I yelled.

Then I remembered that it was Tuesday, the day my mother taught an English class at the Y.M.C.A. where my father was the director.

I stood in the hall, trying to catch my breath, and as always I began to feel small. It was a huge hall with ceilings so high it was as if they would have nothing to do with people. Certainly not with a mere child, not with me—the only child in the house. Once I asked my best friend, Andrea, if the hall made her feel little too. She said no. She was going to be a dancer and she loved space. She did a high kick to show how grand it was to have room.

Andrea Hull was a year older than I was and knew about everything sooner. She told me about commas, for instance, long before I took punctuation seriously. How could I write letters without commas? she asked. She made me so ashamed that for months I hung little wagging comma-tails all over the letters to my grandmother. She

---

5. **George the Third** king of England at the time of the American Revolution

told me things that sounded so crazy I had to ask my mother if they were true. Like where babies came from. And that someday the whole world would end. My mother would frown when I asked her, but she always agreed that Andrea was right. It made me furious. How could she know such things and not tell me? What was the matter with grown-ups anyway?

I wished that Andrea were with me now, but she lived out in the country and I didn't see her often. Lin Nai-Nai, my amah,[6] was the only one around, and of course I knew she'd be there. It was her job to stay with me when my parents were out. As soon as she heard me come in, she'd called, "Tsai loushang," which meant that she was upstairs. She might be mending or ironing but most likely she'd be sitting by the window embroidering. And she was. She even had my embroidery laid out, for we had made a bargain. She would teach me to embroider if I would teach her English. I liked embroidering: the cloth stretched tight within my embroidery hoop while I filled in the stamped pattern with cross-stitches and lazy daisy flowers. The trouble was that lazy daisies needed French knots for their centers and I hated making French knots. Mine always fell apart, so I left them to the end. Today I had twenty lazy daisies waiting for their knots.

Lin Nai-Nai had already threaded my needle with embroidery floss.

"Black centers," she said, "for the yellow flowers."

I felt myself glowering.[7] "American flowers don't have centers," I said and gave her back the needle.

Lin Nai-Nai looked at me, puzzled, but she did not argue. She was different from other amahs. She did not even come from the servant class, although this was a secret we had to keep from the other servants who would have made her life miserable, had they known. She had run away from her husband when he had taken a second wife. She would always have been Wife Number One and the Boss no matter how many wives he had, but she would rather be no wife than head of a string of wives. She was modern. She might look old-fashioned, for her feet had been bound up tight when she was a little girl so that they would stay small, and now, like many Chinese women, she walked around on little stumps stuffed into tiny cloth shoes.

---

6. **amah** woman servant, especially one who serves as a baby's nurse
7. **glowering** scowling

Lin Nai-Nai's were embroidered with butterflies. Still, she believed in true love and one wife for one husband. We were good friends, Lin Nai-Nai and I, so I didn't know why I felt so mean.

She shrugged. "English lesson?" she asked, smiling.

I tested my arm to see if it still hurt from the twisting. It did. My foot too. "What do you want to know?" I asked.

We had been through the polite phrases—Please, Thank you, I beg your pardon, Excuse me, You're welcome, Merry Christmas (which she had practiced but hadn't had a chance to use since this was only October).

"If I meet an American on the street," she asked, "how do I greet him?"

I looked her straight in the eye and nodded my head in a greeting. "Sewing machine," I said. "You say, 'Sew-ing ma-chine.'"

She repeated after me, making the four syllables into four separate words. She got up and walked across the room, bowing and smiling. "Sew Ing Ma Shing."

Part of me wanted to laugh at the thought of Lin Nai-Nai maybe meeting Dr. Carhart, our minister, whose face would surely puff up, the way it always did when he was flustered. But part of me didn't want to laugh at all. I didn't like it when my feelings got tangled, so I ran downstairs and played chopsticks on the piano. Loud and fast. When my sore arm hurt, I just beat on the keys harder.

Then I went out to the kitchen to see if Yang Sze-Fu, the cook, would give me something to eat. I found him reading a Chinese newspaper, his eyes going up and down with the characters. (Chinese words don't march across flat surfaces the way ours do; they drop down cliffs, one cliff after another from right to left across a page.)

"Can I have a piece of cinnamon toast?" I asked. "And a cup of cocoa?"

Yang Sze-Fu grunted. He was smoking a cigarette, which he wasn't supposed to do in the kitchen, but Yang Sze-Fu mostly did what he wanted. He considered himself superior to common workers. You could tell because of the fingernails on his pinkies. They were at least two inches long, which was his way of showing that he didn't have to use his hands for rough or dirty work. He didn't seem to care that his fingernails were dirty, but maybe he couldn't keep such long nails clean.

He made my toast while his cigarette dangled out of the corner of his mouth, collecting a long ash that finally fell on the floor. He wouldn't have kept smoking if my mother had been there, although he didn't always pay attention to my mother. Never about butter pagodas,[8] for instance. No matter how many times my mother told him before a dinner party, "No butter pagoda," it made no difference. As soon as everyone was seated, the serving boy, Wong Sze-Fu, would bring in a pagoda and set it on the table. The guests would "oh" and "ah," for it was a masterpiece: a pagoda molded out of butter, curved roofs rising tier[9] upon tier, but my mother could only think how un-sanitary it was. For, of course, Yang Sze-Fu had molded the butter with his hands and carved the decorations with one of his long finger-nails. Still, we always used the butter, for if my mother sent it back to the kitchen, Yang Sze-Fu would lose face[10] and quit.

When my toast and cocoa were ready, I took them upstairs to my room (the blue room) and while I ate, I began *Sara Crewe* again. Now there was a girl, I thought, who was worth crying over. I wasn't going to think about myself. Or Ian Forbes. Or the next day. I wasn't. I wasn't.

And I didn't. Not all afternoon. Not all evening. Still, I must have decided what I was going to do because the next morning when I started for school and came to the corner where the man sold hot chestnuts, the corner where I always turned to go to school, I didn't turn. I walked straight ahead. I wasn't going to school that day.

I walked toward the Yangtse River. Past the store that sold paper pellets that opened up into flowers when you dropped them in a glass of water. Then up the block where the beggars sat. I never saw anyone give money to a beggar. You couldn't, my father explained, or you'd be mobbed by beggars. They'd follow you everyplace; they'd never leave you alone. I had learned not to look at them when I passed and yet I saw. The running sores, the twisted legs, the mangled faces. What I couldn't get over was that, like me, each one of those beggars had only one life to live. It just happened that they had drawn rotten ones.

Oh, Grandma, I thought, we may be far apart but we're lucky, you and I. Do you even know how lucky? In America do you know?

---

8. **pagodas** temples in the form of a pyramidal tower of several stories

9. **tier** layer

10. **face** dignity; self-respect; prestige

This part of the city didn't actually belong to the Chinese, even though the beggars sat there, even though upper-class Chinese lived there. A long time ago other countries had just walked into China and divided up part of Hankow (and other cities) into sections, or concessions, which they called their own and used their own rules for governing. We lived in the French concession on Rue de Paris. Then there was the British concession and the Japanese. The Russian and German concessions had been officially returned to China, but the people still called them concessions. The Americans didn't have one, although, like some of the other countries, they had gunboats on the river. In case, my father said. In case what? Just in case. That's all he'd say.

The concessions didn't look like the rest of China. The buildings were solemn and orderly with little plots of grass around them. Not like those in the Chinese part of the city: a jumble of rickety shops with people, vegetables, crates of quacking ducks, yard goods, bamboo baskets, and mangy dogs spilling onto a street so narrow it was hardly there.

The grandest street in Hankow was the Bund, which ran along beside the Yangtse River. When I came to it after passing the beggars, I looked to my left and saw the American flag flying over the American consulate[11] building. I was proud of the flag and I thought maybe today it was proud of me. It flapped in the breeze as if it were saying ha-ha to the king of England.

Then I looked to the right at the Customs House,[12] which stood at the other end of the Bund. The clock on top of the tower said nine-thirty. How would I spend the day?

I crossed the street to the promenade[13] part of the Bund. When people walked here, they weren't usually going anyplace; they were just out for the air. My mother would wear her broad-brimmed beaver hat when we came and my father would swing his cane in that jaunty[14] way that showed how glad he was to be a man. I thought I would just sit on a bench for the morning. I would watch the Customs House clock, and when it was time, I would eat the lunch I had brought along in my schoolbag.

---

11. **American consulate** office of the person appointed to aid American citizens in a foreign country
12. **Customs House** building where taxes are paid
13. **promenade** place where people walk for pleasure and to display their fine clothes
14. **jaunty** carefree

I was the only one sitting on a bench. People did not generally "take the air"[15] on a Wednesday morning and besides, not everyone was allowed here. The British had put a sign on the Bund, NO DOGS, NO CHINESE. This meant that I could never bring Lin Nai-Nai with me. My father couldn't even bring his best friend, Mr. T. K. Hu. Maybe the British wanted a place where they could pretend they weren't in China, I thought. Still, there were always Chinese coolies around. In order to load and unload boats in the river, coolies had to cross the Bund. All day they went back and forth, bent double under their loads, sweating and chanting in a tired, singsong[16] way that seemed to get them from one step to the next.

To pass the time, I decided to recite poetry. The one good thing about Miss Williams was that she made us learn poems by heart and I liked that. There was one particular poem I didn't want to forget. I looked at the Yangtse River and pretended that all the busy people in the boats were my audience.

" 'Breathes there the man, with soul so dead,'" I cried, " 'Who never to himself hath said, This is my own, my native land!' "

I was so carried away by my performance that I didn't notice the policeman until he was right in front of me. Like all policemen in the British concession, he was a bushy-bearded Indian with a red turban wrapped around his head.

He pointed to my schoolbag. "Little miss," he said, "why aren't you in school?"

He was tall and mysterious-looking, more like a character in my Arabian Nights book than a man you expected to talk to. I fumbled for an answer. "I'm going on an errand," I said finally. "I just sat down for a rest." I picked up my schoolbag and walked quickly away. When I looked around, he was back on his corner, directing traffic.

So now they were chasing children away too, I thought angrily. Well, I'd like to show them. Someday I'd like to walk a dog down the whole length of the Bund. A Great Dane. I'd have him on a leash— like this—(I put out my hand as if I were holding a leash right then) and he'd be so big and strong I'd have to strain to hold him back (I strained). Then of course sometimes he'd have to do his business and I'd stop (like this) right in the middle of the sidewalk and let him go

---

15. **"take the air"** go outdoors, especially for a leisurely walk or a breath of fresh air
16. **singsong** rhythmic

to it. I was so busy with my Great Dane I was at the end of the Bund before I knew it. I let go of the leash, clapped my hands, and told my dog to go home. Then I left the Bund and the concessions and walked into the Chinese world.

My mother and father and I had walked here but not for many months. This part near the river was called the Mud Flats. Sometimes it was muddier than others, and when the river flooded, the flats disappeared underwater. Sometimes even the fishermen's huts were washed away, knocked right off their long-legged stilts and swept down the river. But today the river was fairly low and the mud had dried so that it was cracked and cakey. Most of the men who lived here were out fishing, some not far from the shore, poling their sampans[17] through the shallow water. Only a few people were on the flats: a man cleaning fish on a flat rock at the water's edge, a woman spreading clothes on the dirt to dry, a few small children. But behind the huts was something I had never seen before. Even before I came close, I guessed what it was. Even then, I was excited by the strangeness of it.

It was the beginnings of a boat. The skeleton of a large junk, its ribs lying bare, its backbone running straight and true down the bottom. The outline of the prow was already in place, turning up wide and snub-nosed, the way all junks did. I had never thought of boats starting from nothing, of taking on bones under their bodies. The eyes, I supposed, would be the last thing added. Then the junk would have life.

The builders were not there and I was behind the huts where no one could see me as I walked around and around, marveling. Then I climbed inside and as I did, I knew that something wonderful was happening to me. I was a-tingle, the way a magician must feel when he swallows fire, because suddenly I knew that the boat was mine. No matter who really owned it, it was mine. Even if I never saw it again, it would be my junk sailing up and down the Yangtse River. My junk seeing the river sights with its two eyes, seeing them for me whether I was there or not. Often I had tried to put the Yangtse River into a poem so I could keep it. Sometimes I had tried to draw it, but nothing

---

17. **sampans** various small boats used in China and Japan, usually rowed with a scull or oar from the stern, often having a sail and a small cabin formed by mats

I did ever came close. But now, *now* I had my junk and somehow that gave me the river too.

I thought I should put my mark on the boat. Perhaps on the side of the spine. Very small. A secret between the boat and me. I opened my schoolbag and took out my folding penknife that I used for sharpening pencils. Very carefully I carved the Chinese character that was our name. Gau. (In China my father was Mr. Gau, my mother was Mrs. Gau, and I was Little Miss Gau.) The builders would paint right over the character, I thought, and never notice. But I would know. Always and forever I would know.

For a long time I dreamed about the boat, imagining it finished, its sails up, its eyes wide. Someday it might sail all the way down the Yangtse to Shanghai, so I told the boat what it would see along the way because I had been there and the boat hadn't. After a while I got hungry and I ate my egg sandwich. I was in the midst of peeling an orange when all at once I had company.

A small boy, not more than four years old, wandered around to the back of the huts, saw me, and stopped still. He was wearing a ragged blue cotton jacket with a red cloth, pincushion-like charm around his neck which was supposed to keep him from getting smallpox. Sticking up straight from the middle of his head was a small pigtail which I knew was to fool the gods and make them think he was a girl. (Gods didn't bother much with girls; it was boys that were important in China.) The weather was still warm so he wore no pants, nothing below the waist. Most small boys went around like this so that when they had to go, they could just let loose and go. He walked slowly up to the boat, stared at me, and then nodded as if he'd already guessed what I was. "Foreign devil," he announced gravely.[18]

I shook my head. "No," I said in Chinese. "American friend." Through the ribs of the boat, I handed him a segment of orange. He ate it slowly, his eyes on the rest of the orange. Segment by segment, I gave it all to him. Then he wiped his hands down the front of his jacket.

"Foreign devil," he repeated.

"American friend," I corrected. Then I asked him about the boat. Who was building it? Where were the builders?

He pointed with his chin upriver. "Not here today. Back tomorrow."

---

18. **gravely** seriously

I knew it would only be a question of time before the boy would run off to alert the people in the huts. "Foreign devil, foreign devil," he would cry. So I put my hand on the prow of the boat, wished it luck, and climbing out, I started back toward the Bund. To my surprise the boy walked beside me. When we came to the edge of the Bund, I squatted down so we would be on the same eye level.

"Good-bye," I said. "May the River God protect you."

For a moment the boy stared. When he spoke, it was as if he were trying out a new sound. "American friend," he said slowly.

When I looked back, he was still there, looking soberly[19] toward the foreign world to which I had gone.

The time, according to the Customs House clock, was five after two, which meant that I couldn't go home for two hours. School was dismissed at three-thirty and I was home by three-forty-five unless I had to stay in for talking in class. It took me about fifteen minutes to write "I will not talk in class" fifty times, and so I often came home at four o'clock. (I wrote up and down like the Chinese: fifty "I's," fifty "wills," and right through the sentence so I never had to think what I was writing. It wasn't as if I were making a promise.) Today I planned to arrive home at four, my "staying-in" time, in the hope that I wouldn't meet classmates on the way.

Meanwhile I wandered up and down the streets, in and out of stores. I weighed myself on the big scale in the Hankow Dispensary[20] and found that I was as skinny as ever. I went to the Terminus Hotel and tried out the chairs in the lounge. At first I didn't mind wandering about like this. Half of my mind was still on the river with my junk, but as time went on, my junk began slipping away until I was alone with nothing but questions. Would my mother find out about today? How could I skip school tomorrow? And the next day and the next? Could I get sick? Was there a kind of long lie-abed sickness that didn't hurt?

I arrived home at four, just as I had planned, opened the door, and called out, "I'm home!" Cheery-like and normal. But I was scarcely in the house before Lin Nai-Nai ran to me from one side of the hall and my mother from the other.

"Are you all right? Are you all right?" Lin Nai-Nai felt my arms as

---

19. **soberly** solemnly
20. **dispensary** place where medicines are available; drugstore

if she expected them to be broken. My mother's face was white. "What happened?" she asked.

Then I looked through the open door into the living room and saw Miss Williams sitting there. She had beaten me home and asked about my absence, which of course had scared everyone. But now my mother could see that I was in one piece and for some reason this seemed to make her mad. She took me by the hand and led me into the living room. "Miss Williams said you weren't in school," she said. "Why was that?"

I hung my head, just the way cowards do in books.

My mother dropped my hand. "Jean will be in school tomorrow," she said firmly. She walked Miss Williams to the door. "Thank you for stopping by."

Miss Williams looked satisfied in her mean, pinched way. "Well," she said, "ta-ta." (She always said "ta-ta" instead of "good-bye." Chicken language, it sounded like.)

As soon as Miss Williams was gone and my mother was sitting down again, I burst into tears. Kneeling on the floor, I buried my head in her lap and poured out the whole miserable story. My mother could see that I really wasn't in one piece after all, so she listened quietly, stroking my hair as I talked, but gradually I could feel her stiffen. I knew she was remembering that she was a Mother.

"You better go up to your room," she said, "and think things over. We'll talk about it after supper."

I flung myself on my bed. What was there to think? Either I went to school and got beaten up. Or I quit.

After supper I explained to my mother and father how simple it was. I could stay at home and my mother could teach me, the way Andrea's mother taught her. Maybe I could even go to Andrea's house and study with her.

My mother shook her head. Yes, it was simple, she agreed. I could go back to the British School, be sensible, and start singing about the king again.

I clutched the edge of the table. Couldn't she understand? I couldn't turn back now. It was too late.

So far my father had not said a word. He was leaning back, teetering on the two hind legs of his chair, the way he always did after a meal, the way that drove my mother crazy. But he was not the kind of person to keep all four legs of a chair on the floor just because someone wanted him to. He wasn't a turning-back person so I hoped maybe he would understand. As I watched him, I saw a twinkle start in his eyes and suddenly he brought his chair down slam-bang flat on the floor. He got up and motioned for us to follow him into the living room. He sat down at the piano and began to pick out the tune for "God Save the King."

A big help, I thought. Was he going to make me practice?

Then he began to sing:

"My country 'tis of thee,
Sweet land of liberty, . . ."

Of course! It was the same tune. Why hadn't I thought of that? Who would know what I was singing as long as I moved my lips? I joined in now, loud and strong.

"Of thee I sing."

My mother laughed in spite of herself. "If you sing that loud," she said, "you'll start a revolution."

"Tomorrow I'll sing softly," I promised. "No one will know." But for now I really let freedom ring.

Then all at once I wanted to see Lin Nai-Nai. I ran out back, through the courtyard that separated the house from the servants' quarters, and upstairs to her room.

"It's me," I called through the door and when she opened up, I threw my arms around her. "Oh, Lin Nai-Nai, I love you," I said. "You haven't said it yet, have you?"

"Said what?"

"Sewing machine. You haven't said it?"

"No," she said, "not yet. I'm still practicing."

"Don't say it, Lin Nai-Nai. Say 'Good day.' It's shorter and easier. Besides, it's more polite."

"Good day?" she repeated.

"Yes, that's right. Good day." I hugged her and ran back to the house.

The next day at school when we rose to sing the British national anthem, everyone stared at me, but as soon as I opened my mouth, the class lost interest. All but Ian Forbes. His eyes never left my face, but I sang softly, carefully, proudly. At recess he sauntered[21] over to where I stood against the wall.

---

21. **sauntered** strolled

He spat on the ground. "You can be bloody glad you sang today," he said. Then he strutted off as if he and those square knees of his had won again.

And, of course, I was bloody glad.